THICKER THAN *Water*

BECCA SEYMOUR

RAINBOW TREE PUBLISHING

THICKER THAN WATER

FANGS & FELONS
BOOK ONE

BECCA SEYMOUR

RAINBOW TREE PUBLISHING

ALSO BY BECCA SEYMOUR

Zone Defense

No Take Backs | No More Secrets | No Wrong Moves

Fast Break

Rules, Schmules! | Facts, Smacts! | Regular Smegular

True-Blue

Let Me Show You | I've Got You | Becoming Us | Thinking It Over| Always For You | It's Not You | Our First & Last | Next For Us

Outback Boys

Stumble | Bounce | Wobble

Stand-Alone Contemporary

Not Used To Cute | High Alert | Realigned | Amalgamated | Under the Blazing Stars

Urban Fantasy Romance

Thicker Than Water | Weaker Than Instinct

For information, contact the author: hello@beccaseymour.com

EDITING: HOT TREE EDITING

COVER DESIGNER: BOOKSMITH DESIGN

PUBLISHER: RAINBOW TREE PUBLISHING

E-BOOK ISBN: 978-1-922359-00-1

PAPERBACK ISBN: 978-1-922359-01-8

"The blood of the covenant is thicker than the water of the womb."
—Matthew 26:27,28

CHAPTER 1

Heat rippled over my skin. The singed scent of hair clogged my ability to track the way out, leaving me momentarily cursing my stubbornness for going this alone. My boss would never let me live it down if I got myself charred to a crisp or killed. At least the latter would mean I wouldn't have to listen to his pompous spiel about following protocol. The dick had it out for me. He had since I'd joined this team three years ago, and despite my success rate on missions, he hadn't taken kindly to the son of the Blackheath alpha joining the Supernatural Investigation & Crime Bureau.

Creaking beams followed by the crash of timber had me blinking hard against the blackening smoke. There had to be a way out. While Brent, my division leader, thought I was foolhardy—or perhaps simply a fool—I had studied the schematics of the lab prior to entering. What I hadn't planned for was Jonas Cartwright to set the damn thing on fire with me in it.

Focussed on pushing my senses beyond the sound of the licking fire and groaning foundations, I closed my eyes, hoping for a ripple, something, anything that would get me out of this situation. Two beats, three, four... but nothing. I could either stay planted, hoping a miracle would happen, or I could act. Neither seemed like a smart move but staying put and being roasted was not an option. The raw heat travelling up my arms, removing my hairs along the way, cried out for my retreat.

Action it was.

In barely a split second, my eyes shifted. While the heightened sight wouldn't help with the smoke, the lights had been tripped by the fire, and I needed all the help I could get.

I cursed up a storm in my head as I raced the way I'd come. With a leap over a toppled cabinet, a swerve away from the licks of fire trailing along workstation dividers, I swore the whole time I would find Cartwright and put him to ground once and for all. The way ahead was blocked, and no barrelling through would solve that. I screeched to a stop. "Shit." I looked left and right, thinking hard about the drawings I'd glanced at ten seconds before entering the lab. Screw Brent and his demands for being well-prepared. I had no doubt my name, Callen, was already a regular curse from him. This would simply give him more ammunition. It was better than him seething my surname, Blackheath, I supposed, but still, ten seconds of my eyes roaming over the layout was as good as studying in my world.

Before I could figure out my next move, a small scrape of metal to my left had me turning in that direction. I seriously hoped I wasn't racing towards more flames, but the sound was distinctive, controlled.

On reaching a hallway I didn't recognise, I stumbled. "What the hell?" At the end of the darkened hallway was a glass door. While smoke spiralled through the space, it wasn't as black, the fire not yet having reached the area. I crouched low to avoid the white smoke, my eyes focussed on the hand scratching against the glass door. Blood smeared with every gentle swipe, the movement slowing down.

No one was supposed to be here. Ignoring the fact that Cartwright had blown my half-arsed recon out of the window and taken me by surprise, there seriously shouldn't have been anyone else on site. An unfamiliar edge of panic flared to life in my chest. This was not good.

I charged towards the glass, stopping short of

barrelling into it to try the handle. It wouldn't have been the first time I'd broken down a door unnecessarily. I didn't want to crash through a glass door unless I had to. While I healed quickly, shards of glass cutting through my skin still hurt something fierce.

Testing the handle with one hand, I hit the glass lower down, trying to get the attention of the person attempting to get out. Their bloody hand peeking out a white lab coat twitched at the loud thud. "Shit," I grumbled. The door was locked. "Hey." I beat against the glass panel harder. It was partially misted for privacy, and visibility was unclear. Unable to tell who was on the other side or whether the smoke had breached the room from another direction, for once, I considered my options.

"Hey." I tried again, my hand smacking the glass harder, not yet intending to break through. "Can you hear me?" Steadying my breath took concentration, but I needed to listen carefully.

"Code." The voice was gravelly. "P-Panel."

I searched quickly and found a panel off to my right. "I need the code." Each word came out calm and clear. Panicking now could possibly get us both killed.

"Five." A cough wracked through him, loud and sounding painful. I squinted, wondering what the hell this guy had been through. "Two. Seven. Seven. Four. Nine."

I hit the numbers as he said them.

"Hash," he finished, and the door clicked, swinging open when the guy fell against it. He landed on the floor.

Unconscious at my feet, the man was sprawled on his front. I tugged him to the side. With no idea where we were, I couldn't simply throw the guy over my shoulder and start charging around, hitting dead ends and burning doors wherever we went. Decision made, I cast a quick glance at the man. Wet blood covered his rich black skin, but his moving chest indicated he was breathing. Barely. Christ, I hoped he didn't die on me. After a final glance, I rushed into the unlocked room. Just because it had been sealed from the inside didn't mean I wouldn't be able to get through another exit.

A door on the opposite side of the room was my target. I headed straight there, spotting vials and another room off to my right. Before I reached the exit, the scent hit me. Blood, and it wasn't from the unconscious lab tech in the hallway. I took a tentative step in the direction the scent came from, bile already churning in my gut.

No. It couldn't be.

Another step forward, and I held my breath, not wanting to believe it could be true.

Wide-eyed, I gasped for breath, then regretted the action immediately. Metallic, familiar, and dead. The combination of the three threatened to buckle my knees. Unable to look away, I stared hard, hating every second. But I had to do this. Flesh, torn muscle, mutilated claws; the image seared itself into my mind. Once there, a shockwave of pain ripped through me.

No.

This time I let my knees go and landed on the floor, my knee finding the blood the same shade of my own. It was her. Hazel. My baby sister.

Her lids were open, her eyes human, despite being in the state of midchange. It made no sense. My brain couldn't join the dots beyond that she shouldn't be here. The last time I'd seen her in person twelve years ago, she'd been over a thousand kilometres away up north in Queensland. She'd still been in the pack, had a child. My niece.

My stomach rolled, threatening to spill its contents.

Nothing made sense.

What the hell was she doing here?

Movement from outside the room caught my attention. It was followed by a cough. Red bled into my vision. Someone knew what the hell had happened, and the guy who'd just regained consciousness was going to give me answers, on his deathbed or not.

Jaw tight, fists clenched, I refocussed on getting free so my brain could function again. Pain beat at my heart, a solemn drum that could easily take me away and lead me to my own destruction. I couldn't let that happen. Wouldn't.

Lucinda.

Agony arrowed through me, soul deep. My niece... where the hell was she? I stormed towards the door and pressed my hand on it. Cold. I nodded in relief. Perhaps the fire hadn't spread this far yet. An overturned metal chair in the corner seemed like my best way out. The cold metal gave a little under my grip, my anger clawing at the surface as sorrow and fury pulsed through me. The metal was strong though, strong enough to break the glass and find a new way out.

Two hard hits did the job, but it wasn't time for relief. A war raged inside me, threatening to pull me in too many directions. Distracted, I took a second to focus. Exit. Retrieve. Retreat. Those three things I could do.

Focussing first on retrieving the man, I hauled him up and slung him over my shoulder. I didn't dare cast another glance at my sister's body. I would be back for her though. The same access code to another door led me to an Exit sign. It opened easily. I glanced through the doorway. Five steps, then the external door to freedom.

And answers.

I set the man's still form on the ground, debating for the barest of seconds whether or not I should secure him. When he stirred, my decision was made. One punch, consequences be damned, and I knocked him out and hardened myself for the next task. Retrieving Hazel's remains was a necessary horror.

After racing inside, I snatched a blanket off an unmade gurney and gently wrapped my sister's mutilated body in the fabric. Red against white. Drips contrasting with crisp folds. Fragmented remains forever embedded in my memory. Pain lanced through me as I lifted Hazel into my arms, then followed the same route to safety. Away from the smoke and fire, and away from immediate danger, I rested the stained sheet doubling as a shroud next to the wounded man. My heart stuttered, sorrow threatening to overwhelm and bring me to my knees.

Sirens wailed in the distance. My saving grace, and the only thing stopping me from buckling. I had to call this in before the fire crew got here, else the mountain of shit I would be in would multiply. I took a moment to place my hand on Hazel and closed my eyes, making her a promise to find out what had happened and to take care of her daughter. My hand came away, leaving a bloody handprint on the blanket I'd used to wrap her body.

I looked over at the lab tech's limp form before standing. He'd been in the room with her. Whether she'd been dead or alive, whether he was responsible or not, he must have answers. I turned and sprinted towards my car, needing to grab my comms.

Once the bud was in my ear, I flicked it on. "Agent Callen, two three five nine, reporting in."

"Location?"

"Northwest of Landing Street. Crandore Laboratories."

"Stand by, Agent Callen."

Static filled my ear as I returned to my sister. The sirens were no longer distant. I estimated thirty seconds before they reached me. I clenched my jaw, wanting to hurry this along. While I needed the engines to arrive as quickly as possible since evidence was burning away while I stood twiddling my damn thumbs, I also needed to make this whole catastrophe official.

"Callen. Man, you're in so much shit. Brent punched a hole in the wall next to your door."

I held back my groan, my emotions and mental state too frayed to deal with Lucas. "Reporting a fire at Crandore Laboratories."

"Oh sh—"

"One unconscious but alive employee." I assumed as

much from the lab coat the guy wore. "And one dead shifter."

"Wh—"

"Just get it in the system. I've got five—"

"All done." Lucas hesitated. "You sound off. What's goin—"

"Meet me at the SICB medical lab?"

"Sure. I'll be there when you get there. I need to tell Brent."

I grimaced. Lucas was a good guy, the best. He'd always had my back, and I'd admittedly put him in the middle of some crazy situations over the time we'd known each other, starting at the academy. Nothing too deep, but I was sure he wished he'd chosen another partner in our first close-combat class. But still, the guy was over a hundred years old and had led a different life before deciding to join the SICB. I figured he was old enough to deal with every decision he made. "Can you buy me some time? Thirty minutes?"

He snorted. "Callen, I'm good, but that's pushing it."

I glanced away and watched the fire trucks pull in, their shouts already filling the burnt air.

"—warpath, for real this time."

The man at my feet stirred, and I glanced down. "He knows I went offline?"

"Did you not hear a word I just said?"

I should have felt guilty, but Lucas knew exactly what I was like, knew what to expect. I took action. Got the job done. And I occasionally played by the rules, just often enough to keep from getting myself fired.

His sigh filled my ear. "I'll do what I can. See you in ten."

"Thanks." I exhaled, relieved I would Lucas would be meeting me.

Ignoring the fire crew beginning to unravel hoses, I knelt beside the stirring body. It wouldn't be long before the human police would arrive, and no doubt before that the SICB as per standard protocol when an incident involved a category 3 facility. My narrowed eyes roamed the man's body. He was bloody, but I couldn't scent my sister's blood on him. With a flick of his lab coat, I exposed his shirt. The same blood stained the blue cotton. A look under the material revealed no wounds. It was strange. There was more blood closer to his chest, to his neck. I tugged his collar out the way and froze. A bite mark, raw, raised, and clear of any blood.

I shot a quick gaze at my sister and then back to the man. Could she have bitten him?

I scrubbed at my face. If that were the case, this had just got a hell of a lot more complicated.

It only took a show of my badge and a few curt

conversations to put both my sister's body and the man's prone form—I may have knocked him out again—in the same ambulance with the instruction to head to the SICB medical lab.

Being in the SICB had its perks, and anything involving supes meant we trumped jurisdiction. I'd shown the arriving human police the bite on the guy, so they'd had no choice but to let me take him.

I followed close behind, having no idea how today's events could have ended in such a mess.

My sister was dead.

I breathed through the pain piercing my chest. While we hadn't seen each other since I'd left my father's pack to start my new life and join the SICB, it didn't mean I didn't love her or hadn't missed her.

We'd kept in contact via email and had even managed a few video calls in secret. It was why I felt like I knew my niece. The whole cloak-and-dagger nonsense surrounding our correspondence was frustrating, but it was what it was. When I'd left the pack, I'd become dead to them, by order of my father. I sneered at the term. *Father*. He didn't deserve such a title of respect. He was a sadistic SOB at the best of times. At the worst, he was a thieving, crooked scumbag who delighted in torturing anyone who dared to oppose his absolute rule.

I engaged my right indicator as we headed closer to

the lab. We were still another few minutes away. While dragging up thoughts of pack life perhaps wasn't the healthiest, it gave me something else to focus on. Once back with my sister and the lab tech, it would take enough of my willpower not to crumble into despair and sorrow. Sometimes the evil of my past was safest.

So yeah, it was a no-brainer that once I was able, I left the pack. There were some people I left behind that made the decision difficult, but I had to escape before my dad and I killed each other. I had no desire to be alpha of the pack, ever, and there'd been no way I could have stuck around for longer than I had. Try as he might to make me into the son he thought I needed to be, he'd failed.

SICB training had been the logical step. Justice and all that was so ingrained in me, despite my dad's attempt to beat it out of me, that I knew the SICB was where I was destined to be. It was the only way I could try to make a change in the world.

My phone buzzed. I pressed the button on my steering wheel, activating the call. "Callen," I greeted.

"I'm here." Mathew Lucas.

"Two minutes out. Any joy with Brent?"

Lucas snorted. "You've maybe got fifteen minutes, twenty if you're lucky, before he locates you, so whatever you're planning, make it fast."

"Got it. Thanks."

"Yep."

The line went dead just as the headlights of my car lit up the entrance to the secure building where the SICB medical lab was kept. *Make it fast.* I mulled that over. I couldn't do much for my sister beyond bottling my sorrow up tight to deal with later. The forensic results would tell me more as soon as they were available. My focus needed to be waking up the guy and figuring out his role. I swept my hand over my face and groaned. I was tired, so beyond tired I was running on what little steam I had left. After a quick rummage around in the debris scattered on the passenger seat, I came away victorious with a high-sugar, high-caffeine drink that I needed to help me push through. I chugged it down before I arrived at the gate.

Showing my badge, passing through the retina and fingerprint scanner, I finally made it to the building. I parked as close to the entrance as I was able, jumping out my vehicle as soon as possible. Not knowing if the guy'd woken or not, I wanted to be there before he could get his wits about him.

I reached the rear doors of the ambulance just as they were opened. My gaze lingered on my sister's prone form for a moment. Bile churned in my gut, and I looked away. *Not yet.* The grumble of a deep voice had my eyes darting to the man strapped to the stretcher.

"W-What?" He moved slightly, but without force. Not enough to put any pressure on his binds. All ambulances were kitted out with a range of supe- and human-friendly paraphernalia, just as EMTs had basic training for a variety of species. It meant that the binds holding him down would take a lot of energy to break free from.

The department doors slid open, revealing Lucas. He nodded at me. "Rooms three and five are free."

I bobbed my head in understanding and directed the EMTs to place my sister in room three, and then followed them to room five. Once free of the EMT staff, and the man securely strapped to the bed, I glanced over at Lucas.

He looked tired as hell too. "Was that...?"

My jaw tightened, and I refused to answer. Lucas, as my only friend in this sorry life I lived, had seen enough photographs of her and my niece. He'd even stumbled in on a few video calls.

"I'm sorry," he started, "about—"

"Nope. We've got fifteen minutes."

He nodded his understanding. "What gives?"

"Grant here was trapped in a lab, covered in blood." I'd finally taken a look at the name tag on his lab coat.

"The same lab I found my sister in." In my peripheral, I saw Lucas nod. "He has a bite."

"No shit."

"Yeah, no shit."

"Your sister's?"

"No idea. It's what we need to find out." Though I supposed when the man woke, he'd be able to confirm that too.

Lucas was a vampire. The only vamp I'd actually come across who I liked. Hell, he was the only guy who I called friend these days. Most ran when they learned my last name. It was why I went by my first name, unlike every other person in the bureau. His vamp skills did come in handy every now and then. Sometimes it beat science. "Can you cross check his blood with hers?" I looked over at him.

"I should be able to. It depends on how recently the bite occurred."

I knew that the shorter time period from the point of bite and wolf shifter's death, the easier it was to determine who the actual person was that made the bite. Plus it would tell us if the person bitten would transform.

Lucas got straight to work collecting a blood sample to taste it. The taste test would forever gross me out, but it came in handy. He then went to do the same to my sister. It left me alone with the man who'd remained quiet since his stuttered one-word question. I stepped to the side of his bed and peered down at his face. His eyes were half-lidded and struggling to open. I saw specks of green in his deep brown irises. High cheekbones aligned perfectly to his nose, and admittedly, he was handsome, beautiful in fact.

"Hey." I tapped his cheek. "Grant, wake up." I tapped again, a little rougher. "Grant, you hear me?"

His eyes finally opened fully, his gaze darting around the room. They didn't fix on anything, which I did not have the time for.

I tried again. "Grant, focus." I clicked my fingers in front of his face. Annoyance threatened to surge forth. Just as it built, the red heat of frustration growing, his eyes met mine, and it diminished. Moss. Green, luscious, and stunning; that was the shade of those specks. I swallowed hard, knowing I really needed to look away. I closed my eyes and turned my head. After a quick breath, I refocussed. There was not a chance I'd let myself get distracted or lost in the eyes of this man.

"Grant?"

His forehead wrinkled, nose scrunching, making him look younger than I'd previously thought. "Who?"

My eyes shot to the badge on his coat, then back to his face. "You not Dr Grant Creaser?"

Understanding seemed to register, and his eyes

widened. "No." He shook his head. "Thatch. Liam Thatcher."

"The tag." I refused to look away this time. I was usually good at scenting a lie, and whoever this guy really was was too important.

He winced when he turned his head. "My neck. What happened?"

"The tag," I pushed.

Frustration flared in his eyes until something else registered. Panic. "Holy shit. I was bitten." He pulled against his constraints. "Get me the hell off this bed. Now."

I pursed my lips, ignoring the unease in my gut and the authority in his words. His panic was affecting me. An urge to release him niggled at the base of my skull. And hell, I did not like one bit that this guy was in distress.

"The tag." I would not, could not budge.

He stopped struggling, and I stilled, breathing a little easier. He slammed his eyes shut and scrunched them tightly before scraping his teeth over his full bottom lip. "Thatch." When he opened his eyes, it was clear he'd centred himself. "Thatcher, SICB Human Division. Five six two nine."

What. The. Hell?

I froze, his words sinking in as he continued. "I can't

give you the details as I'm part of an undercover task force. But I imagine my boss, and likely yours"—I cringed at that—"are probably on their way here now. So…" He expelled a deep breath. "You want to get me off this damn bed before they get here?"

Dull energy thrummed through my weary bones. Brent was going to rip me a new one. I was sure of it. Knowing Thatcher was at least right that my division leader would be here any minute, I released him, my guard up the entire time. It didn't matter how pretty this Thatch was, if he was bullshitting me, I'd take him down in an instant.

Five minutes. It was all I had. "My sister?" I watched him carefully as he sat on the bed while he tentatively prodded his neck. He winced on contact, and I involuntarily shifted my feet. There was no way I was stepping forward to help him. No freaking way.

He tilted his head, giving another slight wince as he seemed to register my question. "Sister?"

I clenched my teeth, needing to control my reaction and the emotion still riding me hard. "There was a woman, a shifter in the lab where I found you. She was dead."

"Sister?" Horror shadowed his expression. "Oh God, I didn't…. Hazel was your sister?" He shook his head.

This time I took a step forward, zero idea of comfort in my mind. Fists formed at my sides.

"Did you—"

"No. Fuck no. She was helping me, or I was helping her." He scrubbed his hand over his face. "I'm not explaining myself well. We were helping each other. She'd been injured, hurt. She was also infected to the point of—" He paused and looked hard at my face. No doubt he saw my struggle for control. "She bit me right at the end, knowing she wasn't going to survive." He closed his eyes. "Fuck, I told her it was okay, that she could. The memories...."

Yeah, the memories.

"Do I have twenty-four hours?"

I nodded, sickness sinking in my gut. Twenty-four hours, and Hazel's memories would start to filter into Thatch's. Nobody, even after years of study and research, had any clue of the whys or the genetic anomaly of how it happened, but it did. It simply was one of the aspects that made wolf shifters unique.

A shifter couldn't make another shifter at the drop of a hat—other than the standard way of good old-fashioned sex between male and female. There was one distinctive exception. A wolf shifter could "gift" their ability or gene to another person. But it had to be by choice. It could also only happen once in their lifetime.

And that was if the shifter was dying and bit a willing human. It defied everything we knew about science, but most significantly, and the aspect that truly was blowing my mind, was that with the wolf shifter's death, their final memories were transferred.

Some thought it was a way to prepare the new shifter for their new form, giving the person a heads-up. Some tended to describe the transition as one of ancient rites, suggesting it allowed the new shifter to avenge their host's death. But that would imply all deaths and bites were a result of murder, which was not the case at all. An old-timer, someone who was at death's door due to old age, was able to pass on the gene via a bite. It was just a bit trickier though, as the timing had to be right.

But still, it defied every rational explanation anyone had. Even more than that, this agent in front of me would start to receive my sister's final memories, and quite possibly a few random older ones too, within twenty-four hours. The memories would solidify the transformation. He wouldn't be able to pick and choose the memories from her twenty-eight years on this planet. It didn't work like that. The new shifter was simply given whatever memories made their way through. They could be old or recent, relevant or not.

From Thatch's reaction and half-arsed explanation,

it appeared as though he was expecting the memories to be related to his investigation.

God, my head hurt. Pressure built behind my eyes and a thud started to grow. It was manageable, barely, but in approximately one minute I was confident it would be fierce—once Brent shouted in my damn ear.

He nodded, remaining silent while we both appeared trapped in our thoughts.

"Thank you."

His voice pushed through the throbbing in my brain. My eyes connected with his, and heat flushed across my skin. My reaction to him was not good. Not one bit. I had no room for attraction on the best of days, but this, in the thick of a cluster of craziness.... My emotions couldn't handle it.

"For getting me out," he explained. "And I'm so sorry about your—"

"Nope." I still wasn't ready to deal. I could stick to the facts, deal with the storm about to burst through the doors, but that was it.

Raised voices had me stiffening. Preparing myself, I took a step to the left and leaned against the wall facing the door. The support at my back was needed. It also brought me closer to Thatch. He watched my movement and gave me a tentative smile before his attention was drawn to the door as it tore open.

"Callen, you've got ten seconds to tell me why I shouldn't fire your pathetic arse right now or—" He slammed his mouth shut, his eyes wide when they landed on Thatch.

Laughter edged its way into my throat. Never, not once in all the time I'd been working under the self-righteous bastard, had I ever known him to shut down quite so quickly. And holy hell, his face paled before heating, his eyes seeming to grow wider somehow. A squeak or something slipped out of my mouth unbidden, but it was enough to turn both gazes to me.

It seemed to give Brent the moment to regather himself as his eyes narrowed at me. His closed mouth seemed to struggle with words, and damn if it didn't lighten my heart for just a moment.

"Thatcher." Brent's voice appeared uncertain. Brent was never uncertain. Ever. He seemed to realise it and physically straightened up. He glanced at Thatch, then at me. But rather than the tyranny I expected him to throw at me, his focus returned to the man a mere metre away from my side. "I don't understand."

My eyes moved to Thatch. His jaw clicked, heat travelling up his neck. He looked pissed off, and I had zero idea why.

"Brent. Callen here one of yours?"

Brent didn't hold back his sneer, exposing his

contempt. "Reluctantly, yes, but his status is always up in the air and can be changed at any time."

There was a subtle shift in movement from Thatch. While I'd caught it, I wasn't sure if the very human Brent had. When his head wasn't planted firmly up his arse, Brent was actually a good agent. He'd never allowed his human genes to hold him back. The knowledge annoyed the crap out of me some days.

The side of Thatch's face was to me. His back molars ground together before he spoke. "Callen"—holy hell, my name on his tongue lifted goosebumps on my arms —"saved my arse tonight. Two years of work was almost wiped out, would have been if he hadn't entered Cartwright's lab, found me, and got me out of there." He didn't shout, didn't stutter, and he certainly didn't mince his words. Though heat flew through each syllable, I didn't think pissed off did justice to the anger rolling off him.

For a moment, I wished I had my phone with me, just so I could have recorded the damn thing. Reliving this moment of Brent behaving every bit the reprimanded kid was epic. Who in the hell was this guy really? Liam Thatcher. I was not buying he was a regular agent in the Human Division. There was no way.

"Callen will be joining me and my task force, starting immediately."

"I what now?" I pushed off from the wall. Unease sat heavily in my chest. "But you've been bi—" I could have smacked myself as soon as I started, and definitely once his fiery eyes landed on me. Within the next few hours, the changes would start and then it was up to him to see how his once human form handled the transition. "I mean, what?" Eloquent to a fault, I didn't even attempt to expand.

Thatch's dark brown-eyed gaze raked over me, those damn specks of green brightening a little under the harsh fluorescents. "I now need you on this."

Any smartarse comments stalled on my tongue as realisation finally seeped its way into my exhausted brain and wrecked psyche. He'd be undergoing the change soon, and while I assumed he knew people who could guide him, Hazel was the one who'd turned him. Her memories would be coming to him soon enough, and even though I had no clue what was going on, that information was enough for me to agree.

I nodded.

"Sir, you can't—"

Sir? What the...?

Thatch's stern gaze was enough to stop Brent in his tracks. But I could see the strain in Thatch's form. He was hurt, exhausted, and I imagined his body was already going through hell. While I was a born shifter, I wasn't ignorant to the way the gene passed on, and sometimes the difficulties.

But before I offered my final words of agreement, I just had to know. "So, who the hell are you?"

Brent groaned while Thatch smirked, and damn if the latter didn't make me not really care who he was one way or another.

CHAPTER 2

THE LIGHTS OF THE CARS MADE ME SQUINT. My eyes were sore, my heart hurt, and my head pounded. While it was probably wise that I wasn't driving, sitting so close to Thatch in the back of the blacked-out SUV did nothing to help me relax. On edge didn't even begin to describe the tension running through me.

My brain wasn't up to it. I'd heard enough to understand the basics of what Thatch had told me. Apparently I had high-level clearance now. Maybe in another life I would have felt proud of that. Today was not that day. Thatch was the head of the SICB ITU—the Infiltration Tactical Unit. It meant he only answered to Durrant, the SICB director, herself.

When I'd indicated that I'd never heard of the ITU in the agency, I was shut down quickly. Apparently that was the point. They were supersecret black ops of humans working with a range of supes. He had a selection of agent identities, like the one he'd given me, that would have checked out. The difference was, he'd given me his real name—though an ID that would go with his Human Division identity. I didn't have the energy to think about that further.

Only three people in the bureau knew who he was beyond his close team. Brent was one of them. When he'd shared that information, my stomach had clenched peculiarly. I put it down to the fatigue beating at me. I needed to sleep. Passing out sounded like bliss.

I glanced over at Thatch. While he sat ramrod straight, his eyes were tight. He was struggling. Selfishly, I wanted a few hours' sleep. Then I could function and deal with what he needed. This whole investigation I'd fallen into by accident when I'd tried to gather intel on a recent drug that had hit the streets—its promise to give vampires an all-time high—had thrown me on a path I could never have prepared for.

It also cost me my sister.

I clutched at my chest, trying to keep the pain at bay, and groaned. It was no good. She was gone, and I still didn't know why. Hell, I'd only managed to spend two minutes with her cooling body before I'd placed a kiss on her head and hightailed it out of there. She deserved more, but it was all I had in me.

Warmth on my hand had me glancing down. Thatch's palm pressed against me, wordlessly offering me comfort. Gritting my teeth was all I could manage, swiftly followed by a small nod. Just a while longer and I could break, and sleep, and make sure my niece was safe.

Exhaling, I stared once more out the window, recognising the area. It was upscale and one of the very few properties with small acreage so close to the city. I'd had no choice but to go with Thatch. He couldn't be alone. Yeah, I wanted answers about my sister, which he was yet to divulge, but it was more than that. I felt compelled to be here.

He moved his hand off me when we turned into an entrance secured by impressive-looking security gates. How on earth did he afford a place like this?

"I know." Thatch's voice startled me. "Ostentatious, right?"

I shrugged. "Perhaps a little."

He nodded. "My family always had a thing for privacy. Plus considering you now know who I am and how important it is for my identity at the SICB to remain confidential, protection is pretty important."

I cast a quick glance at the driver, who'd remained stoically silent the whole way.

"That's Bert." Thatch smiled, and my heart stuttered at the action. Damn, his teeth were crazy white and straight. I mentally punched my junk, wondering why I was fixating on his teeth. "He's been my family's driver for thirty years."

Wide-eyed, I glanced in the rear-view mirror and met Bert's eyes. He threw me a wink. "Oh." I chewed the inside of my cheek, then offered, "Hey, Bert."

"Hey, Callen."

Surprise flickered through me that he already knew my name, but then I reminded myself I'd somehow entered an alternate universe, or the Twilight Zone, or something equally as weird.

After passing through security, we pulled up outside a large brick property. It could have easily been an eyesore, simply because of its vastness. But the structure was tasteful. While on the edge of modern, it somehow managed to look like it had been here for centuries.

Bert exited the SUV and held Thatch's door open. I stepped out the opposite side and dashed around to help Thatch. He was flagging, even more than I was. His posture was stiff, body tense to the point his shoulder muscles looked fit to snap.

"You know, being a shifter comes with advantages."

He glanced at me as I spoke, giving me his attention despite the pain he battled. "Yeah?"

"I have these impressive muscles. I can carry you if you want?" I grinned at him. While humour perhaps wasn't the ideal way of trying to help Thatch, it was my go-to fix in so many random situations. "Bride-style?" I waggled my brows.

A snort escaped him, followed by a cringe and the tightening of his features.

"Okay, okay... no bride-style. Sheesh. You could have let me down gently."

With my arm around his waist, I led him towards the house. Bert had gone ahead to the main door. I expected his staff to file out and wasn't sure if I was disappointed or not when Bert pulled out keys, unlocked the door, and disappeared for a few seconds. A house of this size deserved a housekeeper; hell, a damn butler for sure.

Bert reappeared. "His room is the third door on the left up the stairs. You're best to take the room next to his. The one on his left."

My eyes widened when I figured he was directing me with those instructions. Though I couldn't blame him. The first transformation was notorious for being painful and well... odd. Some apparently were in agony, some became murderous, some behaved like they'd taken a ton of coke. And then there were the horny ones, but I wasn't sure if that was an old wives' tale or not.

I nodded my thanks, and as Bert closed the door

behind us, I almost staggered. The house was freakin' beautiful and strangely immaculate. It had a show-home quality to it, though. While it wasn't cold, it didn't feel personal.

"How you doing there, Thatch?" I asked when he became heavier. I was on the cusp of carrying through with my offer. I didn't know what kind of man Thatch was, but with a guy in authority, and I assumed tough enough to kick arse and take names despite being a human, perhaps sweeping him off his feet wouldn't go down too well.

"Yeah. Just hot, and so tired. My neck…." He winced. "Yeah, sleep and willing this to hurry the hell up is about where I'm at. Just need my feet to stop feeling like lead."

That was my cue.

He grunted and gave a small protest when I scooped him up. His glazed eyes swept over my face, and his mouth lifted into a tired smile. "I'll just say thanks."

"Ha!" I grinned and then focussed on the staircase. "No worries. You really don't weigh much with these impressive guns I have."

He gave a half-hearted laugh and leaned against my chest. I was no stranger to having guys draped over me. I was quite partial to it, in fact, but I tensed all the same. A deep woodsy scent of forests filtered through my senses, and I was beginning to recognise this as a scent distinctly Thatch's. It was refreshing, welcoming even. But still, I struggled to relax with him in my arms. Though knowing I had to put him down in a few short steps didn't especially sit well either.

My addled brain wasn't doing me any favours, for sure. I focussed on that, focussed on just getting through the night. Come the morning, I hoped I could finally start to get some answers.

It took a few minutes to get Thatch settled in his room. I resolutely didn't look around his personal space and tried my hardest not to inhale too deeply. The last thing I needed was the scent of Thatch in my system all night. After having searched the three doors in his large bedroom, I'd discovered one that led to another bedroom suite. It made sense Bert had directed me here. It meant I could reach Thatch quickly should he need me.

Everything was so complicated.

Before I could even think about a shower or sleep, I pulled out my phone. There was no choice but to make this call. I had to know.

The phone rang out five times before a tough feminine voice answered, "Hi, Valerie. Good to hear from you." Disdain filtered down the line. There was a muffled voice, and I figured she was stepping out of the house. Shifter hearing made life difficult when wanting to have a private conversation. Footsteps sounded on the floorboards. A soft closing of an external door. The glass was still loose after all these years and still made that annoying sound as it closed.

Her breathing appeared on the line before her hushed, hurried words. "Why are you calling?" Bitterness laced the question, but I'd long ago given up the will to care. My ma had made her decision the last time my dad had stabbed my thigh with his penknife and she hadn't said a word when he'd poured liquid silver into the wound.

I still had no idea why it hadn't poisoned me. Not because of the silver. Hell, I wasn't a werewolf, but bloody hell... it was liquid silver in a hole in my leg. Perhaps if a vein had been nicked, it would have done the job.

I didn't bother with pleasantries. "Lucinda. Where is she?"

My hackles rose when she was quiet a beat too long.

"I swear to God, you need to tell me where she is now."

"Why?"

"Don't try me, Ma." I took a deep breath to try and prevent my weariness from dripping into my words. She smelled weakness, just like him.

"They left six months ago. Good riddance. That bastard child of—"

"Do not talk about my niece that way. Where did Hazel go? Where did she take her?"

She huffed out a breath. I knew the last thing she wanted to do was talk to me, and it amused me that the three times I'd called in the past twelve years, she'd actually picked up. Even more entertaining was that she kept it from him. I had no doubt that was about self-preservation. "They went down south. Somewhere near the southern bushlands."

"Why there and why leave?"

"How the hell would I know where that hussy of a daugh—"

"Why?" I pushed.

"There was talk of marriage."

My brows dipped in confusion. I hadn't spoken to my sister in about nine months. She hated the pack, our dad, but she'd been safe. Neither of us were quite sure why our father had never laid a finger on her. We were both just grateful. "Hazel? Who to?"

"Both." Her words were blunt, emotionless.

Red misted my eyes. Blood pumped at a rate so damn fast I was sure I'd explode. "What. The Fuck?" My niece was eight.

"To the Crimson Pack out west. They were both due

to go, with Lucinda marrying as soon as she came of age, and Hazel to the alpha's son." Defiance laced her words. Could she seriously not see how every word she said was wrong and oh so disgustingly sickening?

"What is wrong with you? That's your daughter, your granddaughter."

She sniffed as though our whole conversation was an effort to her. "Was."

I froze. What did she mean by that? Did she know about Hazel? Had she, *they* had something to do with Hazel's death, and more to the point, where the hell was my niece? "What?"

"What?" she repeated.

"What do you mean by *was*?"

"The pair of them took off in the night. Billy's daughter told us she'd heard Hazel on the phone about her heading to the southern bushlands. That's all I know."

"Did he look for them?" Ma knew perfectly well who I was referring to, and no way would our father have let her run without consequences, especially if he was selling them off, or whatever the hell he'd been attempting.

"They looked." Disgust slithered through her words, making my skin crawl. This woman was born of hell. There was no other explanation for it. "After a month they gave up. Lennon needed his men back here. As far as I'm concerned, they're both dead." The line cut off.

Nausea swirled in my gut. Anger at them, at me, at my sister, and this whole mess of a situation. There had to be a chance Lucinda was okay. The alternative was incomprehensible.

I struggled to breathe, to keep myself from breaking. I shook my head and stumbled to the en suite bathroom. After getting the shower running, I stripped off and stepped inside, not checking on the temperature. Hot or cold, it didn't matter. I was numb.

Water beat down on me, mingling with my tears. The last time I'd cried was when I was eight. The punishment for that was still engraved in my forearm. Hazel deserved my tears, though. They came steady and silent, filled with sorrow and regret. Head against the tiled wall, I released a heavy breath, fighting to compose myself and trying to regain control. In just a few hours, I'd begin to make sense of everything that had happened tonight and then backtrack from there. It was the only way I'd be able to find Lucinda and determine who had killed my sister and why.

Completely spent, I dried off and headed to Thatch's room, towel wrapped around my waist. Asleep, he seemed restful. It should give me enough time to get some shut-eye myself. I found a pair of sweatpants from his drawers and made my way back to the spare bed. After slipping them on, I crashed down on the soft mattress. It took but a moment to fall into the darkness.

I jerked awake. There was no welcome wake-up call, no hazy memory of what had taken place. Instead, the harsh reality of the morning light brought with it my cruel reality. It also brought with it an agonised "Holy shit" from next door.

Rubbing the sleep out my eyes, I didn't have time to contemplate how many hours I'd managed. It was dawn for sure, but I could have had a full twelve hours and I'd still feel like death. Out of bed, I headed to wash up first. Yeah, Thatch was awake, but he'd have to wait a minute for me to relieve my bladder and throw some cold water on my face. Tasks complete, I stood inside his open doorway.

"How you doing over there?" The distance was deliberate. The change in a shifter could be a crazy one. It wasn't like having a separate entity like a werewolf had. We didn't have an independent conscience.

A low moan travelled the distance of the room before he sat up in bed. "I think I'm alive." Thatch's grimace looked painful. "Hurts like a mother."

I nodded. "Care to clue me in on the direction this is going to go?"

Thatch's gaze narrowed a little before he winced as he pressed his hand to his neck. "What?"

I edged into the room and settled on the soft winged-back chair sitting in the corner. It was comfy as hell. Too long with my butt in this seat and I could easily fall asleep, especially in my present state of mind. "Shifting 101: The Change, you studied that, right? It was a basic part of training."

Thatch sighed, his shoulders moving with the release of breath. "Yeah," he said with a wince. "Pain, anger, or something, right?"

I smirked, but quickly pulled it back, sure he wouldn't appreciate me taking pleasure in the moment. "Or something." It was then my eyes landed on his smooth, bare chest. I cast a glance around the room and found his shirt on the ground. It appeared to be torn. Looked like the strength had kicked in. Perhaps the jump in body temperature too. He wasn't raging either, a relief since he was a big guy. When human, there was little doubt I could have taken him. Now, not so much.

The thought was appealing. Completely inappropriate for a whole list of reasons, but with the way his dark skin almost gleamed in the dawn's light, Thatch's body was difficult to ignore.

"What do you think you need?" I pressed on, not a hundred percent sure of protocol. This was the first time

I'd had to guide someone through the change. The process wasn't as common as human scaremongers made it out to be.

"Painkill—"

I shook my head before he had the chance to finish. "Nope. They won't work. Well, nothing you have here anyway." Bottom lip between my teeth, I contemplated the best course of action. He was in pain, that was certain. I ignored the pissy voice inside my head complaining that it wasn't sex he was after. Horny shifters in the change could be relentless though, or so the stories went. The last thing I needed was to have my dick broken. Plus, I was too damn tired.

"Okay." I nodded as an idea formed. Wide eyes met mine, almost vulnerable looking. I doubted many had seen such a look from this man before. "We need to encourage the change. Get it over with. A bit like ripping the Band-Aid off."

"That's your solution?" He slammed his eyes shut and pressed his hands to his head.

"The sooner we can get rid of the pain, the sooner you can breathe, and the sooner you'll be open to Hazel's"—a zip of agony shot through me—"memories." That last point caught his attention. I hadn't held back my pain. I couldn't.

A short nod followed my words, along with a grimace as he pulled himself off the bed to stand.

"On all fours. It'll be easier." I remembered when it was my first time, fully aware a born shifter didn't have it half as bad.

"How—" The sound of his back teeth grinding together made me wince.

"Eyes on me and listen to my voice, okay?"

He blinked his understanding.

"There's not a wolf inside you ready to pounce free, okay? So there's no freaking out, no worrying you'll lose yourself. You are the shifter. The shifter is you. But it's more primal, works with different senses, different... emotions." It was the best word I could think of to describe how it worked being a shifter. "To find the magic, you don't have to look hard. It's in your veins, in your being. All it's waiting for is for you to instruct it. You have to tell yourself you want to be your other self, your wolf self."

I tugged the sweatpants down so I stood before him naked. Clothes shredded during a shift, and while he still wore some, he was in too much pain for us to worry about them. Plus, his anxiety rolled off him in waves. It was deep and layered with uncertainty.

"Have you seen a shift before?" His nod was slight but enough for me to carry on. "Good," I continued.

"So you know there's no blood or gore, but there is reshaping. It can be uncomfortable and it can be crazy fast." Two seconds was my record, and I was cocky about the fact that I was definitely above average.

"But your first time...." I frowned. "Sorry, Thatch, but it's going to hurt so much you're going to think you're dying." Shit, should I have said that? Perhaps this guidance gig was not my strength. I just needed to get this over with. "Okay. We good?" I clapped my hands together once and gave him a forced smile. If looks could kill, I was sure I'd be dead as a dodo right about now. "I'll be here the whole time. Just follow my lead, watch me take form, then tell yourself to do the same."

I willed the change to come, but this time, I deliberately slowed the whole process down. There was no point in offering a demonstration if he missed the whole transformation by blinking.

My hands went first, followed by my arms, legs. The change then spread through the rest of my body and I moved on to all fours. My view changed. I was almost eye level with Thatch. With my eyes in shifter form, I noticed the green of his even more. They shone bright and brilliant as they raked over me, the sensation caressing my skin. His scent was more pronounced and headier. I would have cleared my throat and shaken my head over my reaction had I been in human form;

instead, I controlled my breathing and made sure I didn't purr at the man. Legit, in wolf-shifter form, I could purr as effectively as a damn tabby.

My large head bobbed at him. He then looked away, and the ripple in the air surrounding his form rolled in my direction. I took in every movement, my gaze wandering the length of him to make sure he was okay. And then he screamed. He bucked. He cried out. And damn if my heart didn't constrict. Thatch's anguish rent the air. My hackles rose, my ears perking. I wanted to go to him, lick him, press my heat against him, do… something, anything to take the pain away. But I couldn't. He had to go through this himself.

Thatch's distress grew as his limbs finally began their transformation. They followed the same pattern mine had. His suffering twisted my gut. Unsure if I could take it anymore, my senses too sharp and alert, I turned human with a simple thought. The change centred me, reminded me that before long, he'd be able to do the same—a blink and a thought and he'd be golden.

I sat close beside him as a whimper escaped his newly formed mouth. The change was almost complete. One last push and he'd be finished. I wanted to cheer and encourage him, remind him of who he was. While I'd known the guy for all of five minutes, to be the head of some supersecret elite task force meant that he must be pretty badass. But I clamped down my words of encouragement. I couldn't distract him.

With one final whimper—this one high-pitched and filled with exhaustion—Thatch's wolf form collapsed. Unconscious, fully formed, and freaking perfect.

Now we just had to wait.

CHAPTER 3

Everything appeared to be going according to plan. Thatch hadn't wolfed out. He hadn't tried to mount me. He was also breathing. I counted each of these things as a successful change.

He'd woken about thirty minutes earlier. Exhaustion had swirled through his eyes as he'd looked up at me, still in wolf form. I'd taken a few minutes away from him to rustle him up something to eat. The energy to change took its toll at the best of times, especially the first few shifts.

He'd all but inhaled the plate of meat I'd set out for him. He was now ready to go. Changing back would be easier. While the discomfort would still be present, he shouldn't be as wrecked. The pain of the transformation would be nowhere near as intense. For that, I was grateful. Selfishly, I didn't think I could handle such turmoil from him again so soon.

I transformed quickly before him, just so I could remind him of the process of how to pull the human form back. Shifters could manipulate the order of their change once they were fully in control. To keep it simple, I pulled my wolf back, encouraging my human form out in reverse order. Slow and steady was my aim, ensuring he could see the movements.

Once in my human form, I smiled. "Okay, Thatch. You've got this. Easy as that. Same process. Visualise your human self, encourage your body to find its human shape. You know your body. Know how you feel in it. Now embrace it."

Riveted, I watched the transformation. In wolf form, he'd been dark and surprisingly sleek. Yeah, huge, which I'd expected, but from the muscle definition in his flank, I could tell he'd be unbelievably fast on four paws. It took two minutes for Thatch to be fully human. While I'd appreciated him as a wolf, his beauty and strength, it was nothing compared to the man before me.

Everything about his physical form screamed perfection. Every toned muscle shaped his skin like a marble statue. He was taut and smooth, and holy mother of God, he was uncut and so big that I almost swallowed my tongue looking my fill.

I had to look away. Had to stop ogling his monstrous cock. My eyes widened. Monstrous. It was accurate as hell, but there was nothing ugly about it.

A groan finally dragged my gaze away. Heat spread across my chest and up my neck. Grimacing, I looked his way, hoping he wasn't going to kick my arse. Relief flashed through me when my gaze landed on him. Bent over, hands on knees, he was breathing raggedly. I was an idiot. While the poor guy was struggling through this life-changing moment, I'd been focussing on the size of him and wondering if I could take it or not.

It was time to pull my head out of the gutter and step up to do my job. At the moment, that included helping Thatch and then working through the memories that would start anytime soon.

I handed him a bathrobe, sure it would take him a while to get over any modesty he still may have from his human life. When he didn't take it immediately, I draped it over him and encouraged him to let me help him put it on. He did, his eyes finally connecting to mine as I stood before him and tied the belt.

His dark speckled gaze searched my eyes. Emotion filled its depth, but since I barely knew the guy, I had no idea what exactly I was seeing.

"Come on." With my hand on his arm, I led him to

take a seat on the bed. Once settled, I retreated to the winged-back chair. "You okay?"

"Yeah." A croak split the word. A quick clearing of his throat, and he ran a hand over his short-cropped hair. "Yeah, think so."

"Has the pain eased?"

He nodded and stretched his neck out. A slow, almost tentative touch to the juncture of his throat and shoulder followed. Wide eyes flared on contact.

"You'll always have the scar," I explained. "But it's healed. Does it feel numb?"

He shook his head. "Sensitive but not painful."

"That's good. Need food, drink?"

White teeth flashed my way before he said, "No, but thanks. I'll have something in a minute." A frown slipped over his otherwise wrinkle-free forehead.

"You okay?" I sat forward, waiting for him to respond.

A nod, and his frown settled.

"Have they started?" Anxiety clawed its way to my chest. This was it. I'd finally get answers.

"Yeah. I think so." As soon as he said the words, he tilted his head and shut his eyes. They squeezed tightly together. "Fuck."

I stood quickly, hurried to his side, and planted myself on the mattress next to him. "What is it?"

He shook his head. "It's confusing, so damn confusing. Everything is jumbled...." His voice hitched, and I reached out and placed my hand on his back. Emotion clogged my throat. This was all too real. I had no idea what he was seeing or experiencing, but the spike of his heart rate set me on edge. The loud thud pounded hard, the sound impossible to miss.

"Breathe." I inhaled and exhaled slowly. "Come on. Breathe with me." Repeating the action, I kept it slow and steady. The last thing he needed to do was hyperventilate. "You've got this." *Think*. Thatch had to take control, find a way of structuring and ordering everything flooding his brain. While he had no control of what came to him, he needed to find a way to not let them overwhelm him.

"Okay." I knelt before him, hands on his forearms. "Eyes on me." When deep brown and green peered back at me, I gave an encouraging smile. "Think about how old Hazel seems, think about the location." He nodded. "Begin to separate them, compartmentalise them. I know from psych training you know how to do that." We'd been trained in all manner of areas, psychology being just one in a long list. While I'd been bored as hell during classes, I begrudgingly admitted it had its uses.

Finally.

"Can you do that?"

Still silent, he nodded.

"Good." I searched my memories, considered what else would help. "Lucinda." Steady. Controlled. The word was as unemotional as I could make it. "Her daughter. She's eight. Use that to help you if anything includes her." With the mention of my niece, Thatch visibly relaxed. Not sure what that meant, I pushed on. It was no use questioning him now. "Six months ago, they ran, the two of them."

"Okay." Steady and a little less gruff, his voice made me smile. He was taking control.

"They headed south, just the two of them, but they must have had help." The latter based on the call my ma had been told about.

With Thatch's eyes still connected to mine, it was easy to spot the recognition in them. *Expressive eyes.* I shook the thought away. Concentration from both of us was the key. I'd missed out on so much of Hazel's life, but I knew enough I could help him.

"How you doing there, Thatch?"

An audible breath escaped him. It sounded relieved. He sat back, and I angled away, giving him some room. "Good." He tilted his head back again, exposing the column of his smooth throat, his Adam's apple pronounced and lickable.

I cleared my throat and stood. My reaction to him

was dangerous. The last thing I needed was to become entangled with the guy who was effectively now my boss. More than that, he stored some of my sister's memories. That was weird as hell.

Returning to the chair, I gave myself a moment to gather myself before turning back to him. "You ready?"

"I am." He surprised me by standing. "Let me get some pants on. Then can we do this after I eat?"

Despite my frustration, I nodded. He'd been through a lot, and this was his call. Emotions and my personal stake should have nothing to do with this. It just wasn't that simple. "No worries. I'll fix something up and meet you downstairs in twenty." I expected he'd want a quick shower after all his body had been through. As delectable as the gleam of sweat looked on his midnight skin, he had to be uncomfortable.

"Thanks." With that, he turned. I followed suit and headed to the kitchen.

The pasta was almost cooked and the veggies all but ready by the time Thatch stepped into the large kitchen. I hadn't heard his descent down the staircase. It was the slight change in air, a small vibration that alerted me to his presence. I was either losing my touch, distracted, or he was simply that stealthy. As a shifter, I had no doubt he would be lethal.

"I found cooked chicken in the fridge and some veggies, so have thrown pasta together."

"Sounds good."

At the sound of his voice, I glanced his way. Deliberately not allowing my gaze to travel the length of him, it was still impossible to not notice how well he scrubbed up. At least six two, he had a couple of inches on me. A deep red shirt covered his chest, leaving very little to my imagination, not that I needed to think too hard to remember what he looked like naked. "Feeling better?"

"Yeah, thanks." He stepped more fully into the kitchen, and I side-eyed him as he pulled out crockery and cutlery. "You want beer?"

My nose wrinkled without thought. "No thanks."

He pressed himself against the counter to my side, his face turned in my direction. "You not like beer?"

"I don't drink." I waited for the questions, the ribbing that so often came from guys in the bureau.

"Water or juice?"

Surprise flittered through me. It was refreshing not to either brush aside jibes or explain myself. Both were laborious, and it wasn't anyone's business but my own. After years of witnessing booze fuelling my old man's anger, I had no intention of ever being held hostage by alcohol.

A smile lifted the corners of my mouth. "Water would be great, thanks."

With a nod, he stepped away and headed to the fridge while I drained the pasta. Once done, I tipped it into the sauce I'd made, along with the veggies and chicken. Two bowls were filled, and we sat at the table. The scene felt strangely domesticated and easy. The thought took me by surprise. Truth be told, I couldn't remember the last time I'd sat at a table and ate dinner with anyone, let alone ate at a table by myself. I was all for eating while standing in the kitchen or with my feet up in front of the TV usually.

"This is good. Thanks."

Wide-eyed, I stared at the empty bowl before him. I was halfway through my bowl, which was fast considering we'd sat a few short minutes ago. "Hungry?" Amusement lit my voice and my gaze jumped to his.

His own humour shone in his eyes. "Yep."

"There's more. I made plenty." As shifters, our metabolism ran high the best of times. His body would need more calories to get through this adjustment period, plus the sheer size of Thatch suggested he'd need more anyway.

He laughed. "Why feed an army when you can feed the Hulk."

I froze, my fork midway to my mouth. Food lodged

in my throat and I gasped, struggling to swallow it without choking.

"Shit." Thatch's large hand made contact with my back once, twice, both times so hard my teeth rattled and had I not been a shifter, a bone or five would have broken. Coughing and spluttering, I finally gathered a breath, my food dislodging from my throat. "Callen, man, you okay?" Gentle circles soothed my back. I'd be bruised there for sure, but they'd fade by the end of the day.

I nodded and pushed my food away. Besides Hazel, not a single person I'd ever met had said that ridiculous phrase before, ever. Sadness clogged my throat. Again. A gentle grip to the back of my neck brought me back to my surroundings. Swallowing hard, I winced at my sore throat.

"What happened?" His thumb stroked my hairline. I relaxed a little at the movement, accepting the comfort he offered.

"What you just said,"—gravel laced my words—"you ever said that before?" I angled my head towards him, disappointed when his hand moved away.

After a moment's confusion, understanding filled his eyes. Lips together, he shook his head slowly. Compassion radiated off him, thick, heavy, and comforting. I wanted to bask in it, much preferring that than the sorrow pressing down on me. "Your sister." He didn't need to ask or clarify. It simply was. This was something I would have to get used to over the days, weeks, or hell, even months we'd be working together. I tried to take comfort from that. It was much better than fighting it and running away with my tail between my legs.

Smiling, I ran a hand over my face before returning my gaze to him. Relief flickered in his eyes when his gaze settled on my mouth. "She always said that, probably from the time she was six. It made no sense at all." I laughed, the sound surprising me as it lightened the heaviness that surrounded me. "Who compares an army to the Hulk?" I snorted, my eyes dropping to his mouth when it lifted into a small smile.

"Well, the Hulk was pretty badass and could beat Superman."

"Nuh-uh, you did not just say that."

"What?" His grin was wide. There was zero innocence in his question or his face.

"You know what...," I croaked, trailing off. Taking a drink of water, I knew it was time we talked. There'd be time to correct him later. We needed to get back to our mission. Thatch had recovered as much as he was able with us under the hammer, and my grief needed to focus on finding Hazel's killer. The chair squeaked when I repositioned it to face Thatch more fully. He mimicked the movement. "You ready?"

"Yeah, as I'll ever be."

That, I could relate to.

"Okay, the op," he started.

My face fell, and I looked down but not quick enough for Thatch not to react.

"Hey." His dark hand rested on my arm. I focussed on the comparison. I had an olive complexion, but next to the depth of Thatch's skin tone... the difference was striking, beautiful, and it made me look pasty as hell. Heck, was I really that pale? "Look at me."

My head jerked up, my brain dragging itself away from the distraction of his hand on my arm.

"I know you want to know more about Hazel."

I winced. "Sorry." Once again, I had to remind myself why mixing personal and work was such a bad idea. Work was messy and complicated, as was life. When the two worlds collided, it was inevitable it would cause a new strand of mayhem and confusion. I could see that so clearly with the involvement of my sister, in addition to the unexpected pull I felt towards Thatcher. "I'm okay."

A smile tugged at his lips. "I can only imagine how difficult this is for you, and we'll get there, I promise. But I need to tell you about the op first. We can then start to make sense of everything. Sound good?"

The man was right. I had no choice but to agree and let him take the lead.

"For two years I've been out in the field focusing on blood trafficking. What started off as a search for illegal blood being sold with traces of LIXER, led me to a whole new lead I never expected."

I nodded. LIXER was a drug that stimulated blood growth in humans to help them be feeders for vamps. It was dangerous as hell, with devastating side effects—hence why it was illegal.

"Eighteen months ago, we discovered there was a link between LIXER and a new drugged blood making its way into the market. This one was used as what we thought was a party drug for vamps." Darkness clouded his eyes, his voice becoming even deeper when he said, "Drugs and bagged blood weren't the only things we found."

My heart seized. Beyond a doubt, I knew that whatever he had to say was linked to Hazel.

"A breeding ground to increase blood supply was located in the southwest of Sydney. Experiments carried out on human women to increase blood-production viability was just one area that was discovered. There was also DNA experimentation to try to create a new blood strand, this one involving shifters, humans, and vamps."

Breath froze in my lungs.

"Mutilations, death... children...." He swallowed hard, anger making the movement audible.

I gasped for breath, my hands clawing into fists. It was too hard to stay quiet, but I had to. I had to let him finish.

"We managed to close down seven facilities. Out of the 78 women and children we rescued, only seven lived."

Nausea swirled in my gut. What the hell were these sonofabitches doing?

I couldn't hold on to my silence any longer. "Lucinda?"

Concerned eyes lined with a furrowed brow met mine. "Her daughter?" He shook his head.

"Yeah, my niece." Despite the control I craved, my voice cracked. "She's eight." While I'd shared this detail with him not so long ago, I had to get him to focus.

Thatch balked, his head shaking more pronounced. "I didn't know about her. I'm sorry. I only knew Hazel for thirty-six hours, if that. We didn't talk about anything related to her life outside. If she'd been there, I would have known about it. I'm sure."

I ignored the icy slither of dread, just as I pushed aside the bubble of hope trying to flare in my chest. That could mean Lucinda had been nowhere near any of this nightmare. She could be somewhere safely hidden. "Her memories." While it was impossible to locate all memories, surely something as significant as Hazel's daughter would have pushed through. The mention of her previously seemed to have helped him take control. The reality wasn't quite like that, but hope could be a brutal, unrelenting emotion. It was also alien to me.

The last thing I'd hoped for was to get lucky with a cute warlock I'd met a few months back in a bar. That hadn't panned out so well. Sometimes I *hoped* that my local Thai takeout would bring back their signature dish, which had been pulled a couple of years back, but still nothing. Hope clearly wasn't something I was used to. The concept had been detrimental to my survival growing up.

Thatch nodded in understanding. He took a gulp of his drink and cracked his neck. The sound made me wince. Eyes closed, his brows dipped low. Not sure if I should prod and attempt to guide or shut the hell up, I pressed my lips together, deciding on the latter for the time being.

Two minutes dragged into five, and I resisted the urge to tap my fingers impatiently on the table. Leaning my head back, I concentrated on breathing regularly and keeping my frustration at bay. If I pushed him, I'd no doubt just annoy him.

Just as the minute turned into its sixth, he spoke, the

depth of his voice loud in the otherwise silent room. "She was caught a while back." I froze, unsure which *she* he was referring to. "I can't tell how long exactly, but more than a month." Thatch's eyes sprang wide and they connected with me. His hand landed on my forearm, the touch calming and settling on my skin without hesitation.

A growl slipped out of my throat, low and deep. I cleared my throat and apologised. As shifters, we allowed our more predatory and protective instincts to sometimes drive us. At times, though, they were hard to contain, especially when emotions were running high.

His smile was tentative. His hand remained, as did the eye contact as he continued speaking. "It was your sister." I slammed my eyes closed in relief, a shaky breath escaping me. "She was taken from the street after finishing work. She was alone." The grip on my forearm squeezed reassuringly before letting go, and I opened my eyes and looked down at the place where I still felt his heat.

Thatch angled his head. "Hazel was definitely worried about her daughter, but not terrified for her."

"That has to mean she's safe, right?"

"I think so, but I can only speculate."

I nodded my understanding. He was right. It would

be easy to jump to conclusions, which wouldn't help us in the long run.

"She was definitely at four different facilities. Not sure if there were more."

"Are any familiar to you?" I asked, wondering if they were ones he and his unit had previously closed.

"Yeah. Three of them anyway." He nodded, and a smile traced over his mouth. "I now know the location of the fourth. It's likely still active. The last facility was Crandore, which was where I met her." Before I could ask for more details, his eyes widened and alarm registered on his face. "Holy shit."

"What is it?"

"Your sister witnessed two experiments where shifters were able to turn a human."

Apprehension arrowed through me. "What do you mean?" I already thought I knew but hoped to hell I was wrong.

"Two semi-successful transformations of humans into shifters."

"Semi?"

"The shifters survived and weren't dying at the point of the bite or during the transition. They changed two women. No men were successfully changed." His brows scrunched together. I could only imagine the complexity of putting together her memories into some semblance of order. "The human women who were turned could only partially shift. Hands and teeth. But they survived."

"Are they still alive?"

He shrugged, frustration colouring his features. "I don't know."

"Why?" My brain struggled to come up with a viable reason why these experiments were going ahead, especially in relation to LIXER and blood farming. "Why would they be wanting to remove the limitations for turning humans into shifters? What could they hope to gain?"

The sound of his back teeth grinding preceded his words. "I have no clue."

It was something we'd have to find out quickly. A surge in shifters created by science could never be a good thing. Who knew what was in the human and shifter's systems for the change to happen?

"Did your sister know someone in the Blue Mountains?"

I searched my brain, thinking back to any slip in a discussion we may have had. "Not that I'm aware of. I left Blackheath a damn long time ago. It meant our calls were limited and rare. Just a couple of times a year." Sadness swept over me, wishing I had done something, anything differently. I'd offered to get her out so many times, and she'd always refused. So why would she leave with the help of someone else? She'd known I had the connections and resources to make it happen.

Tentatively, he said, "Debbie?"

I sat up straighter and tore my phone out of my pocket. "Holy hell. Debbie."

"Who's Debbie?" Thatch searched my gaze.

"She was Hazel's best friend when she was a kid. Her parents died, so her big brother, Grady, looked after her. He mated when he was eighteen and took Debbie and his other sister with him when he changed packs. My father was pissed, threw a stink about Grady leaving rather than bringing his new mate into Blackheath." While I'd been young when it had happened, Grady had been a good guy. He'd left me a contact number for David, the alpha of the pack he was transferring too, promising me if I needed help, I should call. He'd known about the beatings I'd received, the level of cruelty. Everyone had. It was a number I'd memorised and had automatically added to every phone I'd ever had. Some habits died hard.

"You think Lucinda may be there?"

I didn't answer. I couldn't.

The call picked up on the fifth ring. "Who's this?" The voice was gruff, authoritative.

"David Laketon?"

"Yeah."

Relief flooded through me that the number was still active despite all these years. "My name's Callen Blackheath. I was wondering if Debbie or Grady Morton were still—"

"I know who you are." While there was no shift in tone, no welcoming reassurance, he hadn't spat my name in distaste either. I hoped that was a good thing.

"Okay. That makes things easier. My sister, Hazel." I was silent a beat. I could not break or allow my emotion to bleed through. "My niece, Lucinda." I slammed my eyes shut, and the warm reassurance from earlier pressed through me. Thatch's hand was on my shoulder. His touch welcome and grounding. "Is Lucinda there?"

For five long seconds, he was silent. "You not asking for Hazel?"

"I found her yesterday."

"You did?" Relief pressed through the line, evident in those two words.

"You didn't report her missing." Accusation slithered through my words, but even as I said them, I knew they were ridiculous and futile. She'd been on the run. "Shit, I'm sorry. I shouldn't have—"

"It's okay." He was giving me a pass, so unlike many pack alphas I knew. Tiredness spilled into his voice when he said, "Is she alive?"

"No." I shook my head, my eyes swimming, and Thatch's hand squeezed firmer. "My niece."

"She's safe."

Phone still at my ear, my head dropped, my hand covering my face. Tears swam in my eyes unbidden, relief visceral and all-consuming. She was alive and safe. "I—" My voice cracked.

"This is Agent Liam Thatcher of the SICB."

I held my breath and refocussed, grateful to Thatch for taking the phone from me.

"David Laketon." His voice came loud and clear, and I realised Thatch had put the phone on loudspeaker. "Hazel, what happened to her?" The alpha's voice sounded hollow. Grief coloured his words. I clung to the emotion, taking strength from it. It seemed genuine.

"Hazel was taken. We think from the street after work."

David cleared his throat before he spoke. "That would be right. She's been gone for almost a month. She was working at one of our local bars. She'd been working a late shift and never returned to the pack's land." His voice came out as a growl when he said, "You catch the bastards who took her?"

Thatch flicked his gaze to me. I'd calmed a little and collected myself enough to sit upright and focus intently on Thatch and his conversation. "No. But we will. We're closing in." His gaze fixed to mine the whole time. And while he'd been answering David, I heard the promise in his words. "Have there been any more abductions?"

"No, nothing." David sounded frustrated. "She was so careful, knew her father's pack had been looking for her. She had a new identity, kept close, never strayed from the pack's rules."

"Yet she was walking out in town by herself late at night?" I growled the words out, my bitterness unable to be contained. I was all too aware that I should have protected her, kept her safe. Knowing I hadn't done anything to save her... it wasn't something I'd ever forgive myself for. That I hadn't known that she'd left our old pack wasn't a good enough reason.

I should have known.

David sighed. "I know you're upset, pissed, so I'll let your accusations slide, Callen. We're just as angry that she was taken. We assumed it was Blackheath, had the feelers to the ground but haven't heard—"

"It wasn't," Thatch interrupted. "It was a private organisation involved in some nasty shit. Things are precarious for shifters at the moment." I was all too aware Thatch couldn't say much. "Just keep eyes on your pack, females especially, both women and children."

David was silent a beat. Having been around a pack

alpha who would have pulled heads off shoulders if anyone had dared ordered him to do something, I was surprised by David's response. "Yeah, will do. Security has already tightened since Hazel went missing."

"Lucinda?" Her name on my lips was barely above a whisper.

"We sent her with Debbie and her mate, Jason, to a pack a few towns over. Lucinda loves Debbie, so she's okay. We thought it best to move her in case it was Blackheath."

I nodded my relief and let my shoulders drop. "Don't tell her about Hazel, not yet." I blew out a breath. "Can you keep her safe for me?"

"Yes." The word was immediate and absolute.

"I'll come for her." I swallowed hard. "After."

"I can do that," David responded, and relief swept through me, threatening to pull me under with the new emotion.

"Thank you." The words weren't enough to express my gratitude, but they were all I could offer.

"If you need anything—"

Thatch answered for me. "Thank you. We'll call. Please keep the information about Hazel quiet if you can. Be on high alert but not to the point of panic."

"On it." With that, the line went dead.

"You going to be okay?" Both of his hands were on

the silent phone. He turned it around, fidgeting. I concentrated on the action, surprised. Little about Thatch suggested he would ever feel the need to fidget.

"Yeah." I flicked my eyes to his face. "She's safe."

A smile lifted his mouth. "She's safe," he confirmed.

I nodded. "We need to find the bastards who did this and shut down whatever operation it is that they're running." Now that I could focus, knowing Lucinda was secure, determination thrummed through me. It forced its way past the heavy emotion weighing me down, instilling purpose where grief had tried to take residence. "Where do we start?"

The green in his eyes darkened, and I saw a similar determination settling in their depths. "We gather the team and go and tear out some throats."

I quirked my brow at that, wondering if the blood-thirstiness was new. Rather than asking him, a wry grin curled my lips. "Sounds like a plan."

CHAPTER 4

For five days we'd been staring at notes on paper and on the screen. While we'd managed to go into the field twice in that time, we were still no closer to locating Cartwright. Thatch had confirmed Cartwright was a key player, so our mission was directed to tracking the piece of crap down and, I hoped, having the opportunity to beat answers out of him.

"Have you heard from Jenson and Michaels?" It had been a few hours since we'd had an update. There were four operatives in total in the team, including Thatch. The low number surprised me. Jenson and Michaels were a human/shifter combo. They were tracking down a lead we'd found in the lab Thatch had extracted from Hazel's memories. The lab was now closed for good. Another explosion had seen to that. Unfortunately, we hadn't been the ones to detonate the bomb, again. But we had managed to pull a hard drive from the wreckage.

Kent was still working on decrypting some of the files. She was a vampire and a legit whizz on the computer. While she scowled a lot, she was all right, well, for a vamp. Her smart mouth did keep me entertained though.

"Nothing yet. They have thirty minutes before they need to check in. They'll do so by the server, so we'll get the update forwarded to us." Thatch stood and stretched. The movement forced my eyes to travel the length of him. I spent far too long casting an appreciative glance at the exposed skin on his stomach.

Kent's snort had me casting my eyes quickly away and in her direction. Her right brow was quirked high, and she shook her head at me. "Loser," she mouthed, and I flipped her the finger.

It was the fifth time today she'd caught me all but salivating over Thatch. In my defence, he was wearing a super tight black tee rather than one of the shirts I was getting used to seeing him in. And by "wearing," I meant hot damn, that man knew how to wear a T-shirt. It hugged every single hard line and muscle and lifted just the right amount when he angled in certain ways.

Getting a hard-on for Thatch was ludicrous. It was the last complication I needed, and this was beyond *not* the right time. But still, my eyes gravitated towards him at least once an hour. I snorted at myself. Who was I kidding? More like ten times an hour.

"You almost done?" His question made me jump. Kent laughed this time, and I gritted my teeth, forcing myself to ignore her.

"Yeah. There are a couple of things I think are worth checking out." I hit Save on the file, and watched the notification telling me it was safe in the encrypted server.

"Sounds good. We can chat over dinner."

And how *that* sounded was not how I really wanted it to be.

Every moment of the past few days had gone at warp speed, despite the seemingly slow progress. One of the elements that still had my mind spinning, though, was how I'd somehow managed to still be staying at Thatch's. In the room next to his. The one with the adjoining door, where I could hear every damn movement he made during the night, every creak of the bed.

It was messing with my mind and my libido.

Besides the intensity and urgency of the case, I did understand the need to be with Thatch. Every day so far, a new memory slipped into place. He talked through each one. While with each recollection a shard of pain punctured my chest, especially when the memory was personal, it quickly became clear how important it was to help decipher Hazel's memories and their relevance.

But the reality of our grabbing dinner together actually meant us ordering takeout, heading back to his mansion, and talking about the case.

"Okay, sounds good." I offered a chin lift and started packing up the work I needed to take away with me.

"Yo, Callen."

I rolled my eyes. "What, Kent?"

"You know flowers are the usual way to woo dinner dates. Ooh...," she continued, and I heard the shit-eating smile in her voice. I didn't even need to turn to see it. "Or a corsage. That's a thing, right?"

"How old are you again? A hundred and seventy-nine?"

She gasped, but it was all fake. "A hundred and sixty-three, shit for brains. And I don't look a day over twenty-three."

"My finger says goodbye, sucker." I waved my middle finger at her and then looked her way.

Her grin was wide, so much so her fangs peeked out. It was a deliberate flash of teasing. A vampire's fangs weren't naturally on display for the world to see. "Why don't you put that finger to good use tonight, wolf boy." Her eyebrows wriggled up and down.

"I've told you multiple times, I'm all man." I quirked my brow at her. While she'd had moments of riling me up over the past few days, her jibes offered a welcome relief.

She was about to continue, her mouth open to respond, when Thatch's voice cut in. "Children, give it a rest. Callen, get your arse out of here. Kent, get yourself home before Jada calls me again complaining about all the late nights I'm keeping you here."

Heat travelled up my neck. I'd been sure Thatch had left the room, hence me talking crap and not shutting Kent down quickly. I kept my eyes on Kent, who smirked and then pressed her lips together. I knew she was dying to laugh her arse off at me. I shot her the evil eye before turning with my arms full of paperwork and heading to the exit.

God, I hated offices and office freaking banter. Put me out in the field any damn day over this crap. Okay, maybe I was full of it a little, as Kent made me laugh about half as much as she annoyed me, but still, something about her made me slip into a more juvenile me, and I had no idea what to do with that.

I stoically ignored Thatch as we made our way to his car. If I remained quiet long enough, I was confident I could then deftly change all subjects away from the nonsense I was sure he'd overheard. Embarrassment already had me wincing that my attraction to Thatch was so obvious, to Kent at least.

"Pizza okay?"

I sighed, a breath of relief escaping, loud and long. "Yeah. Sounds good."

Once in his car, a different SUV than Bert had collected him in just six days ago, I yawned. My jaw cracked, and I shook my head awake.

"Not sleeping?" Thatch's voice wrapped around me in the confined space.

"I'm getting rest, just waking up a few times is all." I glanced his way and saw him nod.

"Me too."

I didn't tell him that I knew and had heard him awake and restless. "Do you feel the need to shift?" It had been a long time since my shifter-self controlled me or even pulled at me to transition, but I still remembered the more primal part of being a shifter that tended to be a little more vocal when so young. While Thatch had a few years on me, in shifter years he was still a cub. "I can help, be there for you."

It didn't matter that I felt a little uncomfortable around him, completely because of my growing attraction. Instead, it was important he knew he wasn't alone. Since shifting that first night, we hadn't discussed his change. Guilt sank heavily in my gut. Not only did I feel shitty for not seeing how he was handling it, but I noticed his shoulders stiffen at my offer. Yeah, he was getting up, taking charge, had looped the big boss into his change of situation, but he'd had zero breaks or real time to acclimatise to his very personal, very physical changes. They were life-changing. Yet I'd ignored the impact they would have on him.

With his shoulders still rigid, he glanced my way so fast and so briefly, if I'd blinked, I would have missed it. "Yeah, thanks. I think that would be good." Ramrod straight, he looked uncomfortable. "I think I could do with a run." Embarrassment tinted his words, and I frowned.

"That's absolutely okay and normal." I reached out and placed my hand on his stiff forearm. "I should have asked before. I'm sorry." I pulled away, ignoring the disappointment settling in my gut at losing contact. Nothing about this situation could be about me. "Okay." Angling to look at him, a plan formed. "Slightly altered plan." I powered on through, and this time, his shoulders relaxed. "Home. Order pizza to be delivered in an hour. Shift and run. Eat. Then the case." I finished with a nod. There was so much going on for the both of us, just trying to navigate through everything that needed to be done took precision and planning. The thought alone exhausted me. I really needed to stop listening out for him at night and start sleeping.

"That sounds good." With my eyes still directed on his face, I saw his smile. The action sent a thrill through me. Having Thatch happy and not so tense would help the investigation, help us shut down all the illegal shit going on, and help me find the person responsible for my sister's death. As much as that thought sobered me, I also called bullshit, because *sure*, those were the only reasons I wanted to see the guy smiling.

It didn't take us long to get to Thatch's and stand outside. Buck naked. The two of us. Alone. My eyes fixed firmly on his, refusing to travel the length of his exposed skin. "Ready?" I ignored the gravel of my voice. I loved shifting at the best of times, but shifting with Thatch and being able to run alongside him.... Hell, if my wolf had a voice of its own, it would be howling at me to shut up and get a move on. Instead, it was all me and my own impatience that I struggled to control.

While I couldn't see the green in his eyes in the darkness of the night, his gaze still captured mine with ease. "Yeah."

I managed a smile. "Remember what I said before, or do you need me to—"

"I'm good."

Yes, he was.

I pursed my lips together, focussing on the energy vibrating off his body. His excitement buzzed through the air, its scent contagious. Without any more preamble, I shifted. While it wasn't my record, it was fast, my intent to show off just a little. When my wolf eyes gazed up at him, this time having absolutely zero choice but to travel the length of his body, a tingle shot through me. He was wide-eyed, his mouth agape. Yeah, he was impressed. I puffed my chest out and gave a deep yip. He jumped and I grinned, sure I looked manic doing so in wolf form.

Thatch snorted, and he shook his head, his own grin forming on his face. "You were always a show-off."

Heat bloomed through me. Such familiar phrases were getting a little easier. So many small moments of my and my sister's history were slipping out of him, most of them happy. I'd decided it was best to try to embrace those and feel lucky for having them.

"Big head," he mumbled. He followed it up with a wink, and I stepped back, waiting for his transformation to unfold.

Fifteen seconds later, Thatch in wolf form stood before me. Strong and dark, he looked every bit the predator I was sure he was. I'd learned some of his past over our late-night talks, but there was still so much more to discover.

My padded feet edged towards him. Every step I made was confident. While in wolf form, different instincts would surface in him. He was still Thatch, just a hell of a lot furrier and faster. I brushed against him, following my instinct to do so. It was something I would never have dreamed of doing in human form—'cause who in their right mind went around brushing themselves against people? I snorted internally.

He leaned into me as my heat touched his. The connection was understandable, since it was my sister who had turned him. It meant we were genetically of the same pack. We were bonded in some way. Magically, mystically linked. Obviously my lusting after him also had something to do with it.

Content from our touch, I nipped at his flank, then bounded away.

The pounding of his large paws was surprisingly soft behind me. I'd expected him to be swift, but not quite stealthy, considering his size. A quick glance to the rear and I continued forward, doing a loop already around the property. He was barely a metre behind me, his presence familiar. We didn't charge or push our speed or our abilities. Instead, we kept a steady pace, stretching our legs, allowing Thatch to familiarise himself with the power of his limbs.

While his property was large, considering its proximity to the city, it didn't take long for us to loop the border a few times. The welcoming scent of the cooler evening mixed with honeysuckle and the few gum trees he had on the property. The bright stars lit our path, their brother half-moon beside them.

The week had been long and confusing. With grief a constant at my heels and my desperation to get on top of the case—alongside the unexpected attraction I had for Thatch—it was the first real time I'd felt at peace. I shouldn't have waited so long to free my wolf.

The transition usually presented an opportunity to gain perspective and freedom. Despite everything going on, this time was no different.

After maybe fifteen minutes of loops, my legs stretched and satisfaction sliding through me, I led Thatch to the small dam tucked in the corner of his property. Racing towards it, I grinned, leaped, and landed in the water. On contact, I changed forms. My human head broke free of the surface and I laughed, the sound loud in the otherwise still night.

Adjusting to the darkness, my gaze quickly found Thatch's sleek form. A moment later, he crashed into the water. A splash, a ripple, and a few seconds later, he broke free.

His laughter licked at my skin, and gooseflesh popped up.

"Hell, this feels good." His bright grin faced my way, and I quickly mirrored his happiness. The whites of his eyes stood out in the darkness, his gaze steady and directed at me.

"Impressive change there." It was. I didn't rub anyone's ego for the hell of it. He was picking everything up impressively fast. Which made sense. In the few days I'd known him, both in the office and in his home, he was a force to be reckoned with. Controlled, observant, and intuitive.

He ran his hand over his face. "Thanks." His tone was lighter, so much lighter than I'd previously heard it. Thatch in a relaxed state was something special. He kicked away and lay back, floating on the surface.

Averting my eyes from his exposed package, I ducked under and did a few strokes in the inky darkness of the tepid liquid. Once back on the surface, I treaded water, this time behind him, closer to his head. "Feel better after the run?"

"Definitely." His eyes were closed, and just a glint of his pearly whites was exposed. "I feel more relaxed."

Humour lifted my voice when I said, "I can tell."

He opened one eye and peered back at me, angling his head a little under the water to see. "Smartarse."

"I have been known to be one every once and a while." The water rippled when I swirled my fingers. I fixated on the movement. It was a much safer sight than staring at the perfect form of the man before me. "I can't imagine how difficult this transition has been for you." My eyes remained on the water. Dragging my bottom lip with my teeth, I pressed down a little, wondering whether I should push the conversation further. With that thought, I rolled my eyes. It was not in me to hold back, so I had no idea why I thought I could start now. Eyes on Thatch this time, wanting to see his reaction, I asked, "Why did you do it? Say yes?"

With his eyes closed, Thatch looked at peace. I had no doubt I screwed that tranquillity up as soon as I asked the question, but it was something that had been playing on my mind. There were a few beats of silence, just the slight ripple of water making a sound, and the odd cricket in the distance.

The water around Thatch splashed as he moved off his back to face me. Just the tops of his shoulders and his head were above water. "She was the only person left in the facility by the time I infiltrated the night before. It wasn't until the next day, the day of the fire, that I was able to get her out of the cell she was trapped in. She was locked up tight." His eyes drifted away from me, looking into the distant night. "I spent hours the previous night trying to get her out." He shook his head. "She never, not once told me anything personal.

Nothing about her daughter, nothing about her brother being in the SICB, even though I told her who I was.

"Jenson and Michaels were dealing with something for the head office, and Kent was doing everything she could behind the scenes to help me get her out. It was a shitshow."

"They knew you were there?"

"They must have done. The cells and labs were empty. The majority of hard drives wiped clean. We lucked out with the one we managed to get access to."

"But they left Hazel behind." I frowned, thinking back to that night and why I was there. I gave a humourless snort.

"What?"

"And there I was thinking Cartwright had a hard-on for me, when it was all about you."

He quirked his brow at me. "Not sure if I should take it as a compliment that the guy set the fire to kill me."

A wry grin flittered across my lips. "Yeah, I suppose." I'd previously explained to him how I'd got the lead about the real purpose of the lab Cartwright had set up. Thatch had been interested in how Cartwright had let down his guard and left the fragment of a paper trail for me to follow. I just thought Cartwright was a cocky bastard and had made a mistake. Thatch wasn't convinced.

Thatch sobered, his tone lowering. "Your sister was already injured, dying. She'd told me about what she knew, what she'd seen. But even though I spent hours with her, the reality was she drifted in and out of consciousness, and"—he grimaced—"she was in pain the whole time so she couldn't keep her thoughts straight. She left me a jigsaw, so many bits of information that made little sense."

I hadn't realised I'd been looking away, consumed with thoughts of Hazel's last hours and the pain she'd been in, until Thatch's warm hand rested on my neck. "You okay to hear more? I can st—"

I shook my head, relieved when I didn't shake his hand away, relishing in the comfort his warmth and strength offered. "Please go on." This time his hand slipped away. The motion paused, his eyes scanning my face. Perhaps I should have been humiliated that he saw right through me, but I didn't have it in me to care. His hand moved slowly down my arm, goosebumps following his path. His hand stopped when it met mine. I turned my palm upwards and welcomed his fingers, gripping them tightly.

Breath rushed out of me, a reminder that I needed to breathe.

He didn't say anything for a beat. Didn't react. His eyes simply remained connected to mine. With his gaze steady, he tugged me along with him towards shallower water. When our feet touched the soft bottom, he stopped moving and continued with his story. "Kent came through in the end. She's how I was able to get to Hazel. We all knew it was too late. She was physically hurt, her body bouncing between shifts. Even if she hadn't told me, the poison, the chemicals they had pumped her with were killing her."

My jaw clicked as I pressed my teeth together, the bone groaning and muscle throbbing. I was thankful for the minimal light from the half-moon; it allowed me a semblance of anonymity in my grief. While my sister deserved every one of my tears, I was spent. Drained. I needed action, and I knew with Thatch leading the way, we'd take the evil bastards down.

"When Hazel asked if I understood how her last bite worked on humans..." A grim laugh escaped him. "... hell, I understood her intentions immediately. She had so many answers locked away in her mind. She couldn't get to them, not in her condition."

"So you took one for the team." There was no mockery, no indignation in my response. Thatch was... damn... I didn't know what he was. Brave. Stupid. A goddamn hero. "You could have died." The truth of the statement had me flexing my fingers against his. My eyes widened. "Shit, you could have died." Horror edged my voice. It didn't matter that he was before me. Very much alive. Very much okay. "You couldn't have known whether or not her bite would have worked, considering everything in her system." Anger crept into my voice. "What the fuck were you thinking?"

His wide eyes and gaping mouth would have been amusing any other time, but not now. Not with the very real knowledge that he was goddamn lucky to be here, to be okay. I slammed my eyes closed. *He could have died.* Fresh pain, unbidden and confusing as hell swept through me like a tidal wave. What the hell was happening? I shook my head, eyes still firmly shut.

"Hey." Hands cupped my face, steady and large. "Callen." His voice was rough. "Open your eyes." The command was there, pulling at me, urging me to do just that. "I swear if you don't open—"

Two things happened. Both shut him down immediately.

My eyes sprang open, and I launched at him, wrapping myself around his body. My mouth connected with his. The warmth of his lips made me groan, and I pressed against him, opening my mouth. My tongue dipped out, and Thatch's matching groan uncurled a wave of desire, sending it racing through my body. His hand was on my neck, holding tight. I shivered under the contact and brushed my lips against his. One more swipe of my tongue and then I gasped.

There was a metre between us.

Fingers to his lips, he trailed over them, his eyes on me, wide and alert. It was the shake of his head that brought me stumbling back to earth.

Should I apologise? Should I leg it? Hell, should I try again? None of those options sounded right. His chest rose rapidly, almost as quickly as mine. But still, me pouncing on the guy was no doubt the most ridiculous action I could have taken. I knew what I'd been thinking... well, what my damn dick had been thinking.

Embarrassment crawled over me, unnerving and humiliating. After clearing my throat, I pressed my lips together and forced myself to stand straighter. The water sent a new ripple around me. "We should head back so we can finish off—" The whites of his eyes gleamed with how wide he opened them. I twisted my lips, trying not to laugh. This was ridiculous. My *reaction* was ridiculous, as was his deer in the headlights expression. "—so you can finish telling me about the night. The pizza guy's probably wondering where the hell we are too."

His expression shuttered. Not quite casual, not quite relieved, but quite possibly something in between. "I could eat." The corner of his lips lifted a little, his voice guarded.

I snorted. "Yeah. Come on. I promise not to pounce on you." Relief swept through me when a more natural twitch of his lips appeared this time. His cheeks hollowed a little, as though he was trying not to laugh. This reaction I could handle. Distract the discomfort with pointless humour. I was so down for that.

"Perhaps you should walk ahead, or maybe to my side."

A snort escaped. The man had jokes, huh. "I'm sure I can resist your arse." I hoped. God, I hadn't taken a good look at the damn thing, and all I could think about was how phenomenal his backside was in jeans. I cleared my throat. "Erm, yeah. Maybe I'll go on ahead."

His grin did nothing to alleviate my boner.

After a fairly awkward walk back to the house, we arrived to see the pizza boxes on his porch. The security guard must have placed them there. Hungry, I took no time in swiping them off the welcome mat, heading inside. I placed them on the hall table and bounded upstairs, aware I was leaving wet footprints in my tracks. "I'll come back with a towel to clean that up," I shouted over my shoulder. I needed pants. Stat. I threw some jocks on first. There was no way I could go commando tonight, something I preferred when relaxing. Getting changed, I considered how I'd screwed up, and while Thatch had done exactly the sensible thing by stopping the kiss, the rejection stung.

Even though I was sure there was something between us, in reality, I had no idea if that was two-sided or not. I'd thrown myself at Thatch, which was so not cool. Mortified, I considered that I didn't even know if he was into guys. There had been that groan, sure. But truthfully, I couldn't be certain the sound hadn't really been my own. What the hell had I been thinking? I scrubbed my hands over my face, aware I'd already answered that question. Idiotic moments were not something new to me, but still, this seemed like a major one.

A deep breath out, and I shook off the desire and the shame.

Food. Then back to the case.

CHAPTER 5

All was going according to plan. I ignored my grimace, hoping fate wasn't tempted by my assessment. Just like clockwork, the employees punched out, leaving behind a security detail of two. A vampire and a lion shifter. It was an unusual combination, especially as lions were not known to play well with others.

Now it was our turn.

The green light was given. A single word: "Go."

Our team of four moved forward, all at our appointed entrance points. Kent—our eyes—had our backs. Like the genius she'd very vocally professed to be—sometimes four times a day—she'd come up with the goods and got a true lead.

As soon as we entered our access points, I focussed

on my task. The lion. Jenson had the vamp. Thatch ran point on Cartwright, with Michaels as backup.

"Callen, clear in the lobby." Kent's voice, while quiet, was clear. I nodded at the camera in the corner behind the lobby desk, aware she was watching. Instructions and all-clears were given all round. Not needing to hunker down, quick, steady steps took me to the left corridor, towards the front lab. The lion would be positioned there.

I cracked my neck, preparing myself. The aim wasn't to get in a fight. Incapacitation was my goal. Then move on to the server room. Kent, even with her kickarse tech powers, hadn't been able to get through their walls, so I would be grabbing them the old-fashioned way.

The corridor was clear, as expected. I moved forward. Pulse pounding, senses spreading out wide, it only took a handful more steps before I caught the lion's scent. It gave me maybe five seconds to get the job done before he became aware of my presence. "Five," I whispered over coms. The team was waiting for my signal. A timed attack. I charged, sprinting at full pelt, springing off my feet just as the shifter raised his gun. The barest of milliseconds was all I needed to register his safety was still on. A beat later, my fist smashed into the side of his head as I crashed down on him, velocity and height a powerful combo.

Not only that, Cartwright's security detail consisted of paid guns for hire from a disreputable local agency who thought simply being a nonhuman was enough to make them qualified for the jobs.

Fools. And I was glad for it.

"Lion down." I zip-tied the guy's hands behind his back and did the same to his feet. A SICB team would haul him in later for questioning. With the first task complete, I headed directly into the main server room.

"Vamp down" came over the line. I smirked, appreciating the distraction. While I had the computer to work on, anticipation vibrated through me. Waiting was not my strength. It had been enough for me to back down and accept that Thatch was taking point on Cartwright. I'd done so with the grace of a grounded stroppy teenager. Kent had been the first to call me on my petulance. Thatch had looked an interesting combination of disturbed, pissed off, and amused.

When he'd promised I would be involved in his questioning, I'd grinned like a fool and proceeded to shut my mouth.

Memory stick in hand, I searched for the right port.

"Not that one, genius." If rolling eyes had a voice, they matched perfectly with Kent's tone.

I shot the camera the finger, my usual salutation for

Kent, and moved to the correct server. Stick in, I sat at the workstation.

"Cartwright down."

My breath rushed out of me at the sound of Thatch's voice. We had Cartwright. A relief. But Thatch being okay was the cause for my deep exhale. It had been four days since I'd recklessly hit on him. Surprisingly, he'd given me a free pass. We carried on as though nothing had happened. Though the *we* was more him, since I worked hard to ignore my reaction to Thatch and my developing feelings.

Still, we got on, made it work, and now we were one step closer to getting real answers.

I keyed in the details Kent had drilled into me. Movement at the door had me glancing over. Michaels.

"All good?" He stood in the doorway and then leaned against the frame, one foot crossing in front of the other. Michaels was the epitome of smooth and laid-back. It made him deadly. A killing machine wrapped up in a smiling and relaxed human body. I'd read his file, knew his numbers. Being in infiltration made so much sense.

I nodded, eyes back on the screen as I continued with the code. A quick scan, and I hit Enter. "Two minutes."

"Yep."

He waited in the doorway while I finished up.

Hanging around for tech was never fun, but at least I'd managed some action. Despite it being over before it had barely begun. It felt like an age since I'd been away from the constraints of an office and research. If it wasn't for the necessity of the investigation, I would have gone stir-crazy. That, and admittedly Thatch were the only things keeping me tethered and not heading out half-cocked, which was more my style.

"Done." Standing, I released the memory stick and then handed it over to Michaels when I reached him. He secured it away. Together, we headed to the waiting vehicle, passing Jenson, who was talking to the SICB agent who'd arrived. Thatch was in the front seat, hands on the steering wheel. His head bobbed in greeting when I slid in beside him. Michaels jumped into the back and I glanced over my shoulder, seeing Cartwright bound on the metal van floor.

As soon as Jenson joined Michaels in the back, Thatch put the van in gear and pulled away.

NOTHING. CARTWRIGHT HADN'T GIVEN US A thing. Thatch, the epitome of control, stormed out the room. He'd officially lost his cool. Equally terrified and impressed, I stepped out of his way, sure he was going to throw something. New memories hit Thatch daily. Some were inconsequential, some were sweet but random moments of my sister's past, while some redirected our investigation and changed our understanding of events.

There was also the incident a couple of days ago when he made cookies at midnight, courtesy of my sister's recipe. While they were legit delicious, we were both kind of freaked by that development.

Between the scattered flashes of memories and Kent's skills, we'd reached the point of Cartwright's capture. And I'd be damned if we halted here. Cartwright had been one of two lead scientists who'd experimented on Hazel. The second person, a woman, Thatch had a face to, but we had no name and no idea of who she was and how far up the sick ladder of corruption and evil she was. To cut the experiments at the core, we had to find the head of the snake.

The whole team knew Cartwright held either the next clue to get us closer, or quite possibly knew the answer.

"You need to cool off and have me give it a try?" While Thatch had barely stumbled since becoming a shifter, the reality was that with shifter blood running through our veins, it wasn't just our bodies that ran a little hotter. Our tempers tended to also. That Thatch had remained unruffled for so long was impressive, but much more and his composure may slip, and he'd find himself turning.

I didn't know how he'd bounce back from that. A small stumble was one thing, but to allow his anger to dictate his behaviour went against who Thatch was soul deep.

His dark eyes peered back at me. Black had all but bled into the moss green. While the fire running through them caused my adrenaline to spike, I was a sucker for the green and wanted it back. "You've read every file on me, right?" I quirked my brow at him, knowing my words to be true even though he'd never told me himself. "You know every investigation I've been involved with. Every capture and kill. And every successful interrogation I've been a part of."

It would be one hell of a file. I would go as far as saying pretty damn impressive and maybe just a bit entertaining. A smug smile lifted my lips when his shoulders relaxed and he rolled his eyes. My smile turned into a grin. It was the fourth time I'd managed to get an eye-roll out of him. I was keeping score.

The snort from my left had my own eyes rolling. Kent. I swore she managed to get a read on everything and was everywhere. She didn't miss a thing. "What?" I flicked my gaze to her.

She shrugged and pressed her lips together, then shook her head. "Nothing."

I gave her a pointed stare.

"What?" Her brows lifted. "I just read something that was funny is all."

I wouldn't ask. Not interested. Nope.

"What did you read?" I whipped my head to look at Thatch, whose question took me by surprise. His eyes were on me, and a small smile now played on his lips. The arse.

"Well—"

I huffed. "I'll go deal with this and leave—"

"Do you want ABBA?"

Kent's voice stopped me in my tracks. I spun on my heel, eyes narrowed. The sound of grinding teeth echoed in my head. While my gaze remained on Kent, I noticed Thatch wince as his body angled just slightly. We hadn't known each other that long, but after living, working, eating—everything except the one thing I knew we shouldn't be doing but I really wanted to do—together, I could read his tells, gestures, could even begin to determine the subtle changes in his breathing. The one he'd just made meant he was fully focussed on my and Kent's exchange.

Curious, yes, but he wasn't alert.

I released my jaw and ignored the crack that came

with it. "No." Perhaps I should have said thanks to eliminate the suspicion that would grow from me being so abrupt. But this was Kent. She was a bitch of the best kind. Mostly. Instead of engaging, I turned and fled. Hand on the door, I cursed as soon as Thatch's question came.

"ABBA? Do I want to know?"

"No."

"Yes."

Kent and I answered simultaneously.

"O-kay." He released the word slowly. There was no way he was letting this go, and I was surprised as hell that Kent knew but he didn't. Kent had baited that damn hook. And I hated being a worm. Detested it in fact. There was nothing bloody wormlike about me.

"Why are you talking about worms?"

I scrunched up my face, back still to both of them. Thank God. "Nothing." Okay, so I may have grumbled my frustration using my fishing metaphor, but I did not want to think about ABBA. Surely there was a rule or something about what happened in the interrogation room stayed in the interrogation room. Right? If not, it should be a thing. I had no drama going all Brad Pitt on anyone who couldn't follow the rules.

It helped that Brad looked smoking hot doing so. I was sure I could pull it off.

"You want me to get answers from Cartwright or what?" My tone was snippier than intended. I threw Kent an "I'll get you back for this" stare. She flipped me off immediately. I then turned my attention to Thatch, my features softening along with my tone when I said, "I'll get it out of him." There was no way Cartwright was leaving this facility until we had what we needed. Thatch above all others knew that.

His piercing gaze searched my own, and he nodded.

"Thank you." I lifted my lips slightly in an apologetic smile.

"No worries." Thatch tilted his chin towards the door. "We'll be watching."

I bobbed my head and clasped the door handle.

"You can tell me about ABBA tonight." His parting words drifted after me as I pulled the door behind me securely. *Son of a witch.*

TORTURE WAS A FUNNY THING… UNLESS YOU were the one strapped down being tormented by the one person who would do everything in their power to get the truth and the information they wanted. Torture by such brutal methods of hanging genitals, flaying, and waterboarding was a thing of the past. Despite some of the bloodthirsty ways of many of the supernaturals in our world, abusing prisoners was not the way we did things at the SICB. Though, I was sure if I offered one of those alternatives to Cartwright, he might have asked for a switch.

Honestly, my method of interrogation was brilliant in its simplicity. While the ABBA jibe may have stung a little, and perhaps had brought with it a level of embarrassment, after two hours with Cartwright and his words finally pouring out, I was prepared to take ownership of my brilliance... ABBA or not.

I was a certifiable genius. Anyone who didn't think so could screw right off.

I hadn't known what blennophobia was until a few days ago. It was amazing the random information I latched onto when investigating, but it was that one word buried in one of the encrypted files in Cartwright's private document that had stood out to me. Not long after its discovery, I'd asked a bemused Michaels to head out and grab as much slime from Target as possible and a bunch of facial tissues too.

Yeah, Cartwright, for all his sadistic testing and researching, had a very real aversion to slime and snot and anything phlegm-related, it seemed.

Go figure.

I looked smugly at the camera as Cartwright gave me

the location of a third research test facility. After straightening my features and pulling myself back from smugdom, I faced Cartwright. While feeling a tad arrogant in the moment, I deliberately had drawn forth that front. I needed it to help dampen the anger inching across my skin, making me want to scratch, transform, and rip the piece of crap's throat out.

He had yet to tell me anything about my sister's involvement. While I had access to some of her memories, I needed—masochistic or not—to hear from Cartwright directly. I tried to convince myself it would help fuel my need to bring down the whole operation. But perhaps I was a glutton for punishment. I should know it all. Have to hear the harrowing facts.

At the end of the day, I hadn't protected her.

"Please, no more." His cries didn't move me one iota. In fact, I blew my nose and placed the used tissue directly in front of him. I didn't get a fist-pump moment from knowing he was on edge, though. I didn't get an explosion of adrenaline or confirmation that I was on the righteous path. I just wanted all the answers.

My smugness disappeared with a pop when I opened myself to the exhaustion that had been creeping towards me since that first billowing inhale of black smoke. It seemed like a lifetime ago.

Controlling my features not to let my exhaustion

show, I pulled up the plastic chair positioned against the wall so I sat opposite the doc. The room stunk of his vomit, and I couldn't wait to get the hell out of there, but no way was that happening just yet.

"It's time to tell me about Hazel."

His ashen face remained blank a moment as his pupils expanded before resettling. The bastard knew exactly who I was talking about. I just had no idea if he knew who she was to me.

He appeared to tether himself as he shuffled uncomfortably, until something akin to pride registered on his face. My finger jerked involuntarily on my thigh, eager to reach out and kill the man. Within two seconds, his neck could be broken and his involvement would be over. But murdering a guy who was chained down wasn't exactly my style, despite the rage swirling in my gut.

"It was happenchance we got Hazel," he began. A flicker of regret for her loss warred with my relief that her abduction hadn't been a hit against me. "But she made so much possible." It seemed like the sick bastard's pride would be exactly what we needed. He was so focussed on his success, if I could keep him talking, we might get what we needed to shut down this operation for good.

"How's that?" His eye contact told me enough—he wanted an active audience.

"Her blood was nothing we'd seen before." A look of

awe appeared in his gaze. "Hundreds of subjects were tested, but she was the first we were able to reproduce with success, grow and develop a new cell. We managed to find others since, once we'd discovered the ideal genetic makeup that made her blood different."

My brain stuttered on "reproduce." In a jar and blood, right? Ice shot through my veins at the alternative. But when he spoke, horror took form.

"Her eggs and the samples we mutated made her an almost perfect host."

Plastic cracked under my hand.

"Five specimens produced were able to multiply blood supply tenfold. Almost as soon as it was taken, the supply reproduced almost at full count."

Nausea threatened to escape, and the plastic that had broken free from the arm of the chair was all but ground to dust. The room took on a new hue, grey with hints of red. My eyes had shifted.

"We were so close to perfection, but the samples died and quickly. Also, there were some reactions."

A flash of my sister's damaged body flooded me. Every muscle in my body tensed.

"We realised if she got pregnant naturally, if she birthed a female, the—"

I exploded out of the chair. A red mist descended as I reached out, only to falter. Thatch's scent was the first thing to register and bleed through my need for blood. After his scent, the heat of his strong arm around my chest and the hard body against my back reached me. Next were his soothing words. "Come on. I've got you. Let's go."

Tension thrummed through every inch of my wired frame. I didn't know if I could. How could I leave this room with Cartwright still alive?

"You need to come, Callen. Not like this. Let me help you." When he followed up with a soft "Please," I dropped my head in defeat, hating every minute.

With his arm still around my chest, my eyes refocussed. Terror painted Cartwright's features, and while the puddle of piss on the floor gave me some satisfaction, nothing but his incarceration—but more preferably, his death—would whet my need for justice.

Out of the room, Thatch kept us walking until we were outside. The journey was a haze of beeps and the whooshing of automatic doors, and bodies moving out of our way. We didn't stop until he was before me, his hands gripping my shoulders, and grass was under our feet.

Forcing myself to focus, my eyes connected with his.

"I need you to take a big breath, okay?" His piercing eyes held me captive, grounding me.

I nodded and inhaled deeply. The rush of fresh air

immediately helped to clear my mind and filled my aching lungs. Had I really held my breath all the way out here?

"Good." His strong hands were unyielding, and I didn't think it was possible to be more grateful than I was with him before me, helping me keep myself together.

"Fuck." The word rushed out of me, and I dropped my head to his chest. He welcomed the move, his one hand releasing my shoulder and moving to the back of my head.

Thatch remained silent, giving me the time to breathe through the anger whirling through my brain, my veins. Heck, my need to strike, my thirst for vengeance seemed to grow and become an extension of my very self.

With my eyes tightly shut, it was easy to try not to deal with any of it, but Thatch was waiting, people were still dying, and all that meant was that I had to let the justice system do its worst for Cartwright and have faith that it wouldn't let Hazel or me down.

"I need protection on Lucinda," I said as I raised my head and looked at Thatch.

"Done."

Damn, I liked his absolute conviction and support. Through the entirety of this shitshow, of the horror of what we'd uncovered, I readily admitted to myself that if it hadn't been for Thatch, I would have handled Hazel's death a hell of a lot differently. Most likely, I would have charged in guns blazing—again—and would have been on a cold slab by now.

I wasn't ready to smile, but I meant the thank you that I offered him.

Thatch nodded, and as if only just realising his hands were still on me, he dropped them and took a small step back. "You ready to go back?"

"Yeah."

CHAPTER 6

Dressed after my hot shower, I padded down the staircase and made my way to the kitchen. The sound of metal—I assumed pots and pans—travelled from there. My ears perked up in interest. "Wow," I said when I entered the room. "You've cooked?" I didn't mean it to come out as a question, but with smoke billowing out of the oven and steam appearing out of two of the pans on the stove, I wasn't quite sure what was going on.

Yeah, there was that one anomaly of the cookie-making incident, but beyond that, nothing before or since. And nothing that looked like a war zone.

The scent of burnt something registered. I winced, relieved I'd been too distracted to scent it before entering the room. With my gaze spanning the entire mess that was usually Thatch's pristine kitchen, I couldn't help but wonder if this was the first time he had used it for anything more challenging than cookies. "So...." I didn't get any further as Thatch's exasperated glance met mine. I waited a couple of beats before taking a few steps further into the room. "Erm...." I really had nothing.

"Nope."

"Nope?" I questioned. While Thatch was the ultimate control freak, I didn't think his resolve was going to cut it this time. I shook my head and headed over to him. Side by side, we stood before the stove and I peered into one of the pans. My brows scrunched in confusion. "I've got to ask. What's cooking?" I aimed for light, supportive, but instead, humour lit my words.

Thatch swept his gaze at me, and I angled towards him. His jaw tensed, his brain appearing to work overtime if the flicker of his eyes was anything to go by. "Spag bol," he eventually answered.

I gave a single nod before casting my eyes on the oven. It was off, thank Christ, but wisps of smoke still filtered out. "And dare I ask what's been cremated?"

His left eye twitched. "Garlic bread."

I bobbed my head before grabbing a towel and lifting the lid off the back pan. A congealed mess greeted me. "And this?" I clamped on to the inside of my cheeks, trying desperately not to laugh. The more I took in the scene, the more the severity of the catastrophe I saw.

"Noodles."

Pressing my lips together, I held back my snort, determined not to break. Between the red tomato splatters across the countertop and up the doors, the smoke, and the glob of pasta, I was rendered speechless. Yes, there was the whole alpha, control-freak part of Thatch, sure, but this was another level of incompetence that I struggled to get my head around. After stopping and starting a few times to figure out what to say, I settled on "How have you survived all this time?" I shook my head, genuinely bewildered.

His face heated, a deep red beneath his dark skin, and interest sparked in my chest.

"Come on. Spill it."

He cleared his throat and took a few steps away, his backside ending up pressed against the unit. "I usually have Mary, my housekeeper, cook for me at times, and I rely heavily on takeout."

I tilted my head and blew out a breath. This time I didn't hold back my grin. "Okay. So why haven't I seen said cook since being here"—it had been a while, so I was somewhat confused—"and why did you attempt to do this now?"

Red travelled further up his neck. My gaze followed

the journey, mesmerised by its movement. Thatch huffed out a breath and angled his neck back. "I suppose I was trying to do something nice. The cookies were a success."

But they were influenced by Hazel. I didn't need to say my thoughts aloud. Instead, my eyes widened, and when he looked back at me, he appeared decidedly shifty. The heavy pounding of my heart picked up a little. "For me?"

"Yeah."

"Wow, okay." Over the past few weeks, we'd had a lot of takeout, which I'd put down to our crazy hours. We were living and breathing our investigation. Occasionally, he'd pulled meals out of the freezer. I hadn't even considered he hadn't been the one to make them. Yeah, I knew he was well off and came from money, but still. It hadn't even registered. I didn't know if I should ask why. It seemed a little too personal, too delicate, which was crazy. All I knew was that despite my fierce attraction to him and that incredible kiss in the dam, there'd been nothing else between us. So this threw me for a loop.

"With everything that's gone down over the last couple of weeks, I just wanted to do something nice. My gran gave me her recipe years ago, and I haven't had anyone to cook for before." He shrugged. "Yeah, we've made progress, shut down a couple more labs, but I know you're anxious about your niece."

I was. Lucinda now had an agent assigned to her, which helped my anxiety, but I wouldn't relax until this was over and I could get to her. My gut clenched. There was no doubt I'd step up and raise her as my own, but hell if that wasn't another area of my life that I still needed to get my head around.

Warmth spread in my chest when I considered Thatch's gesture. It didn't matter that the kitchen would take a couple of hours to clean up, and probably both pans would need throwing out, or the fact that dinner was inedible. What mattered was the unexpected thoughtfulness in what he'd attempted.

How the hell could I not fall for this man?

At every turn, he had my back. Was there to pick up the pieces of the shit going wrong and celebrate the wins we'd had.

Then there was that kiss.

"Thank you," I managed to say, my voice quiet. "Takeout?" I lifted one shoulder and smiled. "You want to call it in, and I'll start cleaning up?" There was so much more I wanted to say, but I wasn't convinced Thatch would appreciate it. While the gesture was a big one, all things considered, he wasn't a guy who'd appreciate me gushing over the fact.

A smile lifted his lips, his skin calming to its perfect colour. "I can do that."

It didn't take long for the two of us to tidy the kitchen. The pans didn't survive, and the oven would need scrubbing due to the overflow of garlic butter, but Thatch told me his housekeeper would sort it tomorrow when we were at work.

We'd taken a break between cleaning to eat the lasagna that had arrived from the local Italian place. And now, we'd finally put the dishwasher on and headed out the back, soft drinks in hand.

"I've already organised additional training. With how crazy it's been, I'm all too aware of how our usual training sessions have slacked off." Thatch eased into the outside chair and kicked out his legs.

I nodded. "It makes sense. It'll be good to train with the team more. While we've been managing to get by, it would be good to see what they can all handle." I smiled at the possibility. Sparring was always a riot. Before this reassignment had begun, without fail I trained with my old team. It was essential to be able to work as a well-oiled unit. It made me think of Lucas. I really needed to touch base with the guy. Though, being in the ITU meant the truth was tricky, as being low-key was imperative. "Kent trains, right?"

Thatch snorted. "She's deadly, man."

I nodded, a smirk on my face. "I believe that, but shit, she knows how to push my buttons."

"She does have a talent for it." He laughed. "I remember the first time Jenson took her on, thinking she'd be a piece of piss to take down because of the computer genius she is." He shook his head, amusement lighting up his eyes. "He quickly realised just how hard-core she is."

"Do you train with the team?"

"Of course." He looked at me curiously. "Why would you think I wouldn't?"

"Brent."

"Ahh." Understanding registered on his face. "Yeah, I can see he'd keep himself separate."

"Yup. He's a wanker, all right." I laughed when Thatch snorted and covered his mouth. "No spitting. Swallow that shit," I said, the words falling out unbidden. Both of our eyes widened, and heat rushed to my cheeks. I coughed and tried to change the subject quickly. It was so easy to forget Thatch was my boss at times. We were so comfortable around each other. While I'd admittedly said a whole lot worse to Brent and previous bosses, Thatch was the first I'd ever had a boner for. "So, about yesterday's game, huh?" Somehow I managed to hold back my groan at my piss-poor job at a subject change.

Thatch's wide grin spread across his face. "Really?"

I shrugged and smiled before taking a drink.

"Back to Brent," he said, and I glanced at him, relieved he'd given me an out.

It was a few days later when training finally began. After a bust the night before at a raid that had ended up being nothing, the whole team was frustrated and keen to work off some steam.

Heat appeared at my back. While the scent was familiar, it was unwanted, but it was enough to let me know Michaels was going to strike.

I turned swiftly before his fist was able to connect with my head. I raised my arm a fraction and then landed a solid blow to his cheek, following through with a step back and a roundhouse kick.

Michaels grunted and hit the floor hard. Not even a second trickled by before I was on him, forearm to his throat. A gurgle escaped his bloody lips, and he slammed his hand to the ground in defeat.

Grinning, I pushed against him and sprang to my feet. His eyes darkened, reminding me that while we were sparring, he was a fierce-as-hell shifter and I shouldn't forget it.

While I hadn't been on this team for long, I hadn't got to my current position on my pretty looks alone. Yeah, my biceps and canines helped. A lot.

My eyes sought out Thatch's immediately while Michaels sat on his arse grumbling. Thatch's grin matched mine, and I swore heat danced in his eyes. My eyes widened a little. Did he like watching me go at it with Michaels... in a completely nonsexual way, of course. No. There was only one guy on this team who I wanted to do the dirty with.

I pulled in my bottom lip and tasted blood. Michaels was fast. Like crazy fast. Thatch's eyes drifted to my action. *Curious*. There was no point even pretending that the thought of this little training session getting him hot under the collar wasn't getting me amped up. Dangerous, since in a room full of supes, my desire would be scented by every damn nose. Well, except for Jenson, but I'd watched him in action early during a sparring session. Despite being human, he could definitely hold his own.

"Come on, wise guy." I held out my hand to Michaels and then tugged him up once he gripped my wrist. "You good?"

"Yeah." He grinned. "Just easing you into things."

I snorted. "Sure you are."

"Hey, I wouldn't want to scare you away so soon."

"There is that," I said with another snort. "I'm sure you could do some serious damage when you're not whimpering and getting your arse handed to you." I grabbed my towel and slung it around my neck. Michaels had fought fiercely. There was a moment there when I thought he had me. A fact supported by how we'd both broken into a sweat, no easy feat with our shifter metabolism. "Hopefully next time, we'll be training for training's sake and not because I'm a performing monkey."

He nodded, his lips quirking. "Boss man there wanted to see what you've got. Properly, this time."

My gaze sought out Thatch's. "You know, since the boss man over there has been a shifter for, what, five seconds, I'd think he'd be the one who'd need to perform and make sure he can control his wolf." I was totally taunting the guy. And by Thatch's grin, he knew it too.

What could I say? I'd be more than happy to go a few rounds with Thatch. Hot and sweaty. Up close and rubbing all over him. I cleared my throat and thought of vaginas. Immediately, I grimaced, my stomach turning. Yeah, it was a sure-fire way to deflate my masting dick.

Joining the fold of Thatch's special task force had been necessary. And while I admittedly had fallen into the team, it didn't mean my placement was forever. Once this case was over, I didn't know if I would return to Brent's division or not. All I knew for certain was that I wanted to stay, be involved with this kickarse crew. If it meant I had to perform every now and again and perhaps toe the line more than usual, I would try my hardest to do so.

While I was all for going after the bastards behind the drug and the blood experiments with guns blazing and claws sharpened, it was Thatch's common sense and reasoning that convinced me of this way. The team. I couldn't go vigilante, and honestly, I thought we were both surprised I hadn't done so yet. But Thatch could make for a compelling argument when he needed to. I just wished it involved tongues and wanks. Alas, despite the occasional look my way and the out-of-character heat I'd just witnessed, Thatch was all business.

Yeah, I could safely say we were officially friends, but still, it sucked arse. Just not the rimming variety. *Sigh.*

"Callen, stop swooning and get ready," Kent sassed.

I rolled my eyes and threw Thatch a smirk before turning my hard stare on Kent. Her mission in life since I'd joined was to rile me up. The woman was a pain in the arse, and I liked her a hell of a lot.

I saw the barely there twitch of her index finger, but it was all I needed—well, that and the slight shift in the air. I ducked low and crouched, my leg stretching and swiping at Jenson. I spun, punching Michaels in the balls before jumping and landing my fist in Jenson's gut. He gasped and hit the ground.

I made a mental note to buy them both a drink or three later.

In today's session that Thatch had orchestrated, we

were instructed not to hold back. There was no chance of that.

The lights shut off, pitching us into blackness. This was new. I quickly centred myself, shifting my eyes to my wolf's. Outlines sharpened into focus, and two figures tentatively made their way towards me.

A thrill shot through my body, and while I was a cocky son of a bitch most of the time, this wasn't going to be pretty. The likelihood was that I was going to get my arse handed to me.

Unless... this was over in the next twenty seconds.

I attacked.

In just five moves, the two were groaning on the floor. The lights flicked on, and I repositioned out of my defensive stance. My eyes adjusting, turning once more human, they landed on the two men at my feet. I winced in sympathy. Maybe I owed them dinner too.

"Need a hand?" I offered.

"No," Jenson groaned. "We're good."

"Speak for yourself," Michaels added. "Shit, Callen, you had to go for my junk. Twice." He continued to moan while lying on the mats, holding his balls.

"I would say I'm sorry...." I offered him a friendly smile.

"Yeah, yeah, I know." Michaels winced. "No holds barred."

I grinned. Michaels was a good agent, despite my ability to take him out so efficiently. My nostrils flared in awareness. Shifting my eyes to the side, my gaze settled on Thatch, arms crossed and looking proud as hell.

"Are you next?" I challenged, my head bobbing up and down.

He stepped towards me, and I refused to swallow at his closing proximity. When he paused less than an arm's length away, he grinned and leaned in. The scent of the woods and Thatch was heady. It was distracting and comforting. I was barely aware of the guys leaving the training room.

With his mouth next to my ear, it was even more difficult to concentrate, especially when he said, "I think it's best we don't spar in public."

Holy balls. There was no stopping the audible swallow this time around. My eyes snapped to Thatch's when he leaned back with a smirk on his face as he stepped away from me.

No, he didn't. Did he? "What the hell?"

His smirk became a full-blown smile. Immediately the wings took flight in my gut, and there was no point even thinking about vaginas to get myself under control. Nothing was going to work.

"Get changed," he shouted over his shoulder just as he exited the room. "You stink!"

Slamming my mouth shut, I stared wide-eyed at the empty doorway. If the bastard was playing with me, I.... Shit, I had no idea what.

With a quick crick of my neck side to side, I looked up to the off-white ceiling. Damn, this place really needed a fresh coat of paint. Nope, staring at the walls wouldn't do anything to ease the ache in my sweatpants either.

With no other choice, I headed to the showers, hoping like hell the place was empty by the time I got there. I didn't think any of the guys would appreciate hearing me jacking off.

After probably fifteen minutes too long in the shower—admittedly, rubbing one out may have been involved—I headed into the main area. I winced when I saw Michaels walking a little bow-legged, pressing an icepack against his crotch. "Dinner's on me," I called out to him.

He grunted, not bothering to look my way before he hollered, "I also expect a bottle of the good stuff in my locker come morning."

I groaned at that. Not only was Michaels a shifter who had a huge appetite, but his taste for booze leaned towards the expensive side. "Your balls should have healed by now. Call yourself a shifter?" I quipped, earning me a flip of his middle finger. Jenson snorted at that. "Maybe you should help him kiss it better," I shouted at Jenson. He was wide-eyed for the barest of moments, surprising me, until his face shuttered and his eyebrow cocked.

"Doesn't he wish," he scoffed.

"Rack off," Michaels shouted, his supernatural hearing picking up Jenson's words despite being in a different room. "You're the one who wishes."

I heard the grumble but wasn't sure Jenson picked it up. It sucked to be human, I was sure. With a shrug, and perhaps spending too much time mulling over if there was anything deeper in the jibes between Jenson and Michaels, I made my way to Kent.

"What's cooking?"

She cast me the barest of glances, though still managed a withering edge to it. "Just finalising intel on a new place Thatch wants to hit tomorrow."

I nodded and reached out to the box of barbecue-flavoured Shapes I spotted. After opening the box and the enclosed wrapper, I scooped out a handful and shoved them in my mouth, munching loudly.

"Do you have to be here for that?" She shot me a look that would make weaker men wilt.

"What?" I mumbled, deliberately letting a few crumbs fall from my mouth. There was no denying I knew how to piss her off. It helped that I was bored and ready to head out, even though it wasn't all that late.

She sighed. Impressive, since she didn't breathe. "Thatch said he wanted to see you when you got your arse out of the shower from whacking off to him."

The dry biscuits caught in my throat. Hacking, I coughed, trying desperately to breathe, in the process spraying the biscuits in a good metre radius around me. Mortification attempted to rear its head but breathing seemed a bigger priority at the moment.

"For fuck's sake." There went her sigh again as she leaned over and smacked me on the back. I shoved forward, flying into the counter, still managing to keep hold of the chair somehow. Pain warred with the relief that I could finally gasp for air.

"Bloody hell," I croaked. "I think you cracked my spine." I eyed her as she shook her head, returning to her computer screens.

"You're such a limp dick, I swear. I have no freakin' idea what he sees in you."

That had me pausing, my ears ringing, though I wasn't sure if it was from lack of oxygen, the pain from her hit, or the possibility of her knowing whether Thatch actually liked me. "What?" I managed, calming my breathing and tentatively reaching around and rubbing my sore back. "Did you have to hit quite so hard?"

"You're welcome for helping you breathe."

"And piercing my lungs with my now broken ribcage," I mumbled.

Even only seeing the side of her face, I knew she rolled her eyes again, but I also saw her lips twitch. She loved me. Thought I was awesome. She just wasn't quite prepared to admit that aloud. And that was okay. She would.

"So..." I edged closer to her. "What exactly does the hunk of a boss man see in me?"

"You sound a little desperate there, Callen."

Meh. There was no denying it. "And?"

She opened her mouth to speak, but I froze, becoming aware of Thatch's presence. I angled my head in his direction.

Despite this, she continued, all of us fully aware she knew he was in the room. "He wants to lick your Zooper Dooper."

I visualised the long, thin iced pole.

Holy shit on toast. Okay, so not quite what I was expecting. "Actually," I said, reacting immediately, trying to take control of my mortification, "It's more like a Cyclone." At that, she cast me a bemused glance. "You know, the Paddle Pop—not only long but *thick*." Her amusement should have been enough to get me to stop, but I was too far gone. "Just to be clear," I shouted in the air, directing it at Thatch, but not quite brave enough to look at him just yet. "My Zooper Dooper is not skinny." I pointed a look at Kent and this time found her grinning. It was the first time I'd seen her genuinely amused and embracing it.

I also didn't miss the "For shit's sake," from Thatch.

"And," I continued, "you know I run hot, not like you icy vamps."

At that, Kent rolled her eyes. By this point I was worried she'd get eye strain or something if she kept at it. I wondered if she could get workers comp for that.

"Callen."

Thatch's voice stopped me, which was probably a good idea. Screw mortification. When challenged, it was always best to roll with it.

"Yep?" This time I glanced at him, fixing a shit-eating grin on my face.

He shook his head and exhaled loudly, his cheeks puffing out at the gesture. "Just get your arse in my office." With that, he turned on his heels and walked away. I jumped up to follow, leaving Kent's laughter behind and Michaels adding, "Did that really just happen?"

"Hell yes. Boss man is so screwed."

My smile grew impossibly wide. *I bloody wish.*

Before I reached Thatch's office, I shook myself off, trying to push away my lusty thoughts. From what Kent had said, more intel had come in and the next day, there was something planned. It didn't take much to get my mindset back into the job. How could it not when the risk to my niece was so real?

I sat down in the chair facing Thatch's desk. He was already sitting, a bunch of paperwork surrounding him and his screens angled so I could see.

"We've received intel about a raid on a shifter children's home."

All humour screeched to a halt. I sat bolt upright, my eyes steady on Thatch until he indicated I should look at the screen. Five children's faces stared back at me, of varying ages between ten to fifteen, if I had to guess, and all girls.

"You suspect it's our mark?"

"Yeah." He exhaled, exhaustion swirling in his eyes and present in his voice. "With all the labs Cartwright gave up now being closed, we expect them to be scrambling. Not only for secure labs but also for more subjects."

A frown dipped my brows, and I leaned back, trying to get my thoughts together. "Why aren't they lying low? They know we're on to them, know we're getting closer.

They can only stay a step ahead for a short time before we catch up and take them down." Conviction lit my words. I believed every word I said. We'd be taking them all down. Now we needed to do that even faster to save the five girls they'd abducted. Anger pulsed through me when I considered how terrified they must be.

"Based on what Cartwright said and our successful raids, I think we have to assume they're close to what they started on Hazel." He eyed me warily, no doubt wondering how I'd react at that news. "This whole thing is a mess. They seem to be involved in so much shit, so many drugs, so many levels of experimentation; it's the reason why for two years I've been working on the damn thing. Shutting shit down as fast as I could, but it's still not fast enough." The sound of his jaw grinding would have been enough to tell me he was struggling, but it was the gruffness in his voice that concerned me more.

He was going to lose it. I couldn't let that happen.

"But you have something for tomorrow that Kent's working on." I made it a statement, ensuring he didn't hear any doubt in my words. "The cluster of chaos that they're involved in, the extremes of what they're involved in, why they are in the first place don't matter for now. Our focus is these girls, getting them out and making sure they're safe." I paused briefly, long enough to distract Thatch from his anger.

"What are you thinking?"

"They're getting sloppy." My grin bordered on sadistic. "When did the girls go missing?"

"At some point during the early hours. We're approximating ten hours."

"They're panicking, getting sloppy. Have they ever done anything like this before?"

Thatch's shoulders visibly relaxed a little as he said, "Never. Always off the streets. Often the homeless, people walking home late at night, the occasional mother and daughter heading to the car after a recital or something, but never like this. Certainly not enough to immediately raise the red flag so quickly." The smile that tipped his lips was thin, but he was no longer feeling as helpless. "Sloppy *and* arrogant."

My mouth quirked a little at that. Reining it in, I asked, "Why can't we move until tomorrow?"

He sighed. "We're still searching for hard intel. There's a lot of talk, but nothing yet concrete. I'm about to call a meeting in thirty, and I expect us to be moving early hours in the morning."

"So no sleep tonight?"

"Nope. I'm giving everyone five hours to get some rest on site, and then we'll debrief two hours before we're set."

"And how about you?" Concern filled my voice. I

understood better than anyone how significant it was to win this one. Get the girls back safely. But that didn't mean Thatch could work on fumes alone.

"What about me?"

I shook my head at him, not at all surprised by his inability to ensure he was looking after himself too. While it made him a good guy and excellent at his job, it also brought with it risk. And that, I wasn't down for. "You and rest."

"I'm all good."

"No, you need to get some downtime too. Everything will be a waiting game until tonight, I expect." I glanced at the clock. It was only just gone midday. "After the meeting, I'll take four, then tag, you're it."

He looked set to argue until his phone rang. He answered it, his eyes still on me. I heard a man's voice down the line. *"We're down to two locations. Should have more in a couple of hours."*

Thatch immediately responded. "Send the specs to me for both. Good job, Jamison."

"You got it." I heard fingers hitting a keyboard down the end of the line. *"Okay, should be good to go, handsome."*

I froze while Thatch shifted uncomfortably in his seat, his eyes, which had been peering at his computer screen, flicking up to meet mine. He coughed, the sound awkward and forced. "Thanks, Jamison. Let me know when you have absolutes."

"You've got it."

Without responding, Thatch ended the call, his eyes now back on the screen, seemingly resolute in not looking my way. Meanwhile, the last few moments of their conversation had been muffled by the deep pounding of my heart. It was loud and fierce, so much so I had to channel my breathing to get myself together.

Handsome? What the ever-loving—

"Check these out."

I shook my head and stood, grateful for the distraction. Green was not a good colour on me. Yeah, it may match his eyes, but that dread swirling in my gut, the familiarity I'd heard in the man's tone, and Thatch not shutting him down.... Nope, I did not like it one bit.

"We have the blueprints of the two possible targets."

I stood behind him, trying my hardest to calm my breathing and the erratic pace of my heart, knowing he'd be able to hear it if he concentrated. And all this without allowing myself to inhale his scent. Proximity was always a struggle with Thatch at the best of times. That added to the jealousy churning in my gut didn't make for the best of situations.

"Do you want to take a look at this one?" He

pointed at the screen, and I quickly refocussed, getting back to the mission. "This one's down at Pier's Head."

I bobbed my head. "You've got it. Send them on over." I stepped away and began to turn. His voice stopped me.

"Let's head into the conference room. That way we can bounce ideas around while I focus on the second location at Madison Rock."

"Got it."

"Meet you in five. I'll get the memo out to everyone to meet us there in twenty-five."

"Got it, boss man." I winced a little at that and refused to look in his direction. Distance was going to be as impossible as unwanted, truth be told. But reminders of why I was here and our roles in it would have to work.

There was too much at stake for bullshit.

CHAPTER 7

I'd managed three hours of sleep and then had frogmarched Thatch to a room to make sure he followed suit. He did so with the expected grumble, but when he'd appeared back in the conference room just over three hours later looking at least a little refreshed, my shoulders had eased.

One of many things I'd learned about Thatch over the past few weeks was that he rarely prioritised himself or his needs. I'd taken it upon myself to make sure that wasn't always the case. There was no point analysing the whys of it either, since my reasons were obvious.

Surprise hit me whenever he didn't fight back too extremely. Yeah, he complained, but he let me get on and take care of him, often in the smallest of ways. Most probably because it shut me the hell up. Whatever his reasoning, it reduced my worry a little, and the rest he'd managed was no different.

A few hours later, we had the confirmed location of Pier's Head, a plan for extraction, and a secondary team on standby. The logistics of such things due to the anonymity of the team blew my mind, but for years they'd had this gig, had multiple aliases even with the SICB that worked.

Thatch was taking point. I was moving in with Jenson through entrance point B, while Michaels had Thatch's back.

There was no chance of a large, loud hit. Not with the girls at risk. And there was certainly no room for mistakes. We had heat signatures on seven in the east of the old factory building. Three more were to the west, and eight to the south, which was where Jenson and I were entering.

Armed with IH darts rather than live rounds due to the nature of our rescue mission, I double-checked my weapon, ensuring the IH setting. I was sure all of us would have happily gone for kill shots, but with so many bad guys on the move and us still not 100 percent sure of the girls' location in the premises, the immobilising tranq darts would have to suffice. They were instant acting and got the job done.

"Quiet and swift." Kent's calm voice filtered through our comms.

I nodded at Jenson, who gave me a chin lift before, together, we edged towards the entry point we'd selected.

With no heat signatures evident in the small room, we'd chosen the large window. Jenson pulled out the WGS knife, a small, sharp, laser-edged blade that was engineered specifically for getting our arse through locked windows quick.

"Got it," Jenson said, indicating for me to grab the left of the glass so we could safely place it on the ground.

Once positioned, I checked out the room, my shifter vision cutting through the shadows. "B clear," I whispered. Jenson bobbed his head, no doubt looking for heat signatures via his thermal imaging goggles. We were both inside a moment later, as were Thatch and Michaels, the former giving the all-clear.

I focused on what I could hear. There was movement a few metres away, likely in the next room, which Jenson confirmed with "Four to the right." I bobbed my head in understanding.

Gun positioned, I edged towards the open doorway, scenting the air as I went. The distinct scent of a tiger shifter was present, but other than that one, I could only smell humans in close proximity. The tiger would be on us before we knew it, so it was necessary to work fast.

As soon as Jenson gave me his signal that he was in position, we made our move.

Stepping out of the room, Jenson going low and at my heels, I took in the four guards. Immediately I targeted the shifter with two fast-fired darts. His eyes flared, not a sound escaping his gaping mouth before he slumped to the tiled floor.

By the time he was down, a second man was following suit, courtesy of Jenson's quick trigger finger, and I pointed at a young, blond-haired guy who fumbled with his weapon. The human didn't even have enough time to brace himself for my next dart before he collapsed.

The final guy seemed to snap out of his surprise, gun raised and mouth open. The dart between his eyes would leave a hell of a sting. My lips twitched as I looked at Jenson, throwing him a wink, impressed with his shot.

We edged to the next door and stood opposite each other. I glanced at Jenson in anticipation. He indicated four again, but this time that he expected them to be the girls.

My heart spiked and I worked hard at controlling it, at the same time scenting. Definitely shifters. But just four.

A moment later we were in the room, my eyes

zeroing in on the four girls. All four pairs of eyes widened at seeing us, a frightened sob coming from behind the gag of one. A girl, the oldest of the group by the look of it, tugged the whimpering child next to her tight to her side, while her gaze didn't stray from mine.

I didn't need to check that Jenson was guarding the door; he knew his job. We'd extract these four via the window, Jenson sending the signal to Kent to gather the second extraction team to collect the girls from us. Jenson and I would continue looking for the last girl while Thatch and Michaels took out the rest of the bad guys.

With my pointer finger to my lips indicating quiet, I edged towards the frightened girls. Crouching before them, I whispered, "Name's Callen. We're going to get you out through the window in the next room, okay?" I spoke directly to the eldest. When I received a terrified nod, I reached out slowly and removed her gag.

Relieved as hell she didn't scream, I smiled at her. "Where's the other girl?"

The shifter child shook her head and whispered, "T-They took her a w-while ago."

"To someplace else or is she still here?"

"S-Still here. I h-heard a metal door."

"I'll find her."

Her eyes filled with tears. "She's my b-baby sister."

Her words hit me hard, and I fought like hell to keep myself in check. "I'll find her and get her back to you." I didn't dare promise, but I'd do everything in my power to save the girl. I only hoped she was still alive. "All four of you, I need you to be as quiet as possible and follow me, okay?" My eyes roamed over them, receiving a small nod from each. "Jenson over there will make sure we're all safe, okay?"

Unsheathing a small knife at my ankle, I reached out and sliced through the heavy-duty zip ties shackling their hands and ankles, while the eldest girl helped the two younger ones remove their gags, mumbling to them softly that they'd be okay.

Once on their feet, I took the hand of a girl with bright blue eyes. "Come on then, sunshine. Let's get you safe."

She nodded immediately, and in a line connected by holding hands, we raced to the next room, skirting close to the walls and aiming for stealth, surprisingly easy with the shifter girls. At the window, I spoke into my comms. "Callen extracting four at point B."

"Meadows at point B." It was the warning I needed before his head came into view.

I gave him a quick nod and picked up the first girl, passing her over into the open arms of Meadows, a guy

I'd never met, a human. The fourth girl, the one who'd been so brave, clung to me a moment, squeezing tight. I swallowed hard. "I'll find her," I said next to her ear before passing her through the window.

"Point B extraction complete," Meadows said before backing away into the darkness.

Swinging myself around immediately, I made my way to Jenson in the next room. I gave him a chin lift, indicating all was well. He didn't exhale in relief; neither of us could, not until we found the final child safely.

After finding our way to a steel door and clearing out a few more guards, we took a breath while I hit my comms. "Callen on comms. What's your position, Thatch?"

His response was immediate. "At your six."

My chest loosened, knowing all the rooms must be clear beyond the space behind the steel door. That, and Thatch was unscathed. A moment later, I sensed movement from him and Michaels. Then they were beside us.

"Just four accounted for. One moved this way not long ago. No rush though. I think we're still good."

"Jenson and I will focus on the remaining girl," I whispered.

Thatch's voice was low when he responded. "Got it. We've got your backs and will shut the place down."

Jenson tried the handle. It turned without sound and he eased open the door. The room was bright.

Thatch instructed immediately, "Kent, lights."

Within a second, the power cut out and we moved in, separating into our pairs. I took in as much of the space as possible. Movement and a grumble off to my right signalled a person, while from a little further back came a feminine voice. "Sort it immediately." She sounded frustrated, tense.

I allowed myself a moment of relief that we still had the advantage until it was cut short by a shouted, "Shit, Danny isn't answering. Get out—"

The man's voice stopped abruptly, I hoped from an IH dart from Thatch or Michaels. I heard the rush of movement before I saw it. Vampire. But the sound wasn't aimed in our direction.

"At your three o'clock," Jenson said, no longer whispering.

Immediately glancing in that direction, my gaze landed on the missing girl strapped to a contraption that had me seeing red. My focus zeroed in on her and getting her out. I couldn't let the worry for Thatch threatening to seep in distract me.

"I've got her. You get the woman."

"On it," he responded.

He separated from me as I raced towards the young shifter. Unconscious but with a heartbeat, she looked pale and far too young to be caught up in anything of this magnitude. I surveyed the needles protruding from her arm and the straps tying her down. Just as I reached out, I heard snarls and scraping metal, followed by an agonised cry. With my gut threatening to turn and my heart close to beating free out of my chest, I released the young shifter's limbs and carefully removed the needles, pressing a gauze I grabbed off the table to her arm.

Her breathing continued in a steady rhythm, dramatically different to my own. "Jenson, report?"

"Got her." His voice was tight, but there was no doubt that if this woman was the other doctor Cartwright had mentioned, we were so close to the end.

"I've got the girl. Let's go."

Not daring to reach out to Michaels or Thatch, as soon as my eyes landed on Jenson with a woman thrown over his shoulder, I manoeuvred the girl into my arms and hauled arse. "Kent," I said en route, "two coming out. Doc's unconscious. Last girl's also out of it. Make sure medical is on standby."

"Head out the front. There's a team waiting."

"Got it." Trying not to jolt the slight girl in my arms, I slowed down just as I approached the door. Before I could reach out, it opened, the same guy, Meadows, at the door.

"I'll take her." He reached for her, and I readily handed her over. Any other time, I would have been eager to see her safely in an ambulance, but with the fight still raging between the vamp, Thatch, and Michaels, I needed to get back there.

"Thanks." With a quick turn, I dashed back through the steel door, finding Michaels pulling himself up off the floor and Thatch flying through the air. Eyes wide and fear crashing through me, I pulled my gun, switching off IH. As I shifted my finger, the vampire snapped his gaze to me. His eyes were shot through with red, nothing I'd ever seen before.

I pulled the trigger, emptying the round. Each bullet missed its mark. The vamp moved so fast he outran a bullet. *What the hell?* Pausing, the vampire tilted his head. The sound of feet headed in our direction. As if that was his cue, he spun on his heel and charged the concrete wall, breaking through the barrier as if it was no thicker than cardboard.

"Out the back," I hollered, trying to redirect the help coming our way. It worked, the sound changing direction. My plan to do the same cut short when Thatch's groan sliced through the air. Following the scent of his blood that had also registered, I went to my knees before him.

Anger fought worry for dominance as my eyes arrowed in on the metal rod protruding from his side, a few inches left of his belly button. With my hand pressing against his chest as Thatch started to come to, I prepared myself for battle. A hurt shifter could likely lash out or simply react and try to jump up, potentially doing lasting damage. No way could I let that happen to Thatch. He'd already been through enough.

"Michaels." My voice was steady despite the anxiety clawing through me.

His groggy moan was his response.

"You doing okay, man? What do you need?"

Thatch's eyes rolled behind his lids, and I held on to him a little firmer.

Michaels's grunt was followed by "Yeah. Took a whack to my head. Nothing else. All good."

Relief had me taking a deep breath. "Okay, good. Get your arse here then and call the EMTs in."

"Fuck. Thatch?"

"They're on their way," Kent said through the comms.

"Yeah. He'll be o—"

Wide, panicked eyes peered back at me as soon as

Thatch came to. His chest twitched under my hand. A loud inhale through his nose came next, and he glanced away from me, his head moving, searching almost frantically.

"Hey, there." My voice brought his attention back to me. "Thatch, you're okay. Just focus on me and take some slow, shallow breaths, yeah?" Miraculously, calm laced my voice, and I willed my heart rate to slow. "We need help to get this out of you safely, okay, so that means keeping your arse still and letting these guys"—I tilted my head to the crew who'd just entered the room, assuming they were the EMTs Kent had sent—"do their thing, then we can get you patched up and let the new awesome shifter healing do its magical mojo shit, yeah?"

When the right side of his mouth tipped up into a smile, despite the pain registering in his eyes, I was sure I was going to start stroking his face inappropriately and whispering sweet nothings to him. It took everything in me to not do that.

When I'd seen his body thrown like a ragdoll by that jacked-up vampire and then registered his pain, despair had hit me harder than I'd thought possible. Without a doubt, Thatch meant more to me than a boss or a friend. And while I hadn't been fooling myself to the contrary, I had convinced myself that something between us could wait until this investigation was locked up tight. But his prone form, the scent of his blood, the fear in his eyes... all of that had hit me harder than a freakin' bowling ball.

Losing him....

I shook my head, a flash of emotion taking flight inside me.

A gasp of breath and a wince followed Thatch raising his hand to me. Wide-eyed, I realised his intention and leaned over a little, allowing his palm to cup my cheek. "I'll be fine," he croaked. "The magical mojo shit will start working soon." He coughed and groaned loudly, his hand falling and landing on the steel pole in his side.

It was enough of a wake-up call for me to say, "Okay, hero. Paws off, and no getting handsy while we're in public." I cast a glance to the young EMT, a panther shifter by her scent, crouching next to me. I threw her a wink. "It's a problem, I know. When I come in such a spectacular package as this..." I shrugged, then focussed once more on Thatch, whose eyes shone from his most recent movement. "... it's no wonder even the big man in charge gets the feels."

The woman blushed while Thatch groaned and Kent said, "You made me lose my damn appetite."

"Will you stop?"

I froze and looked at the iced tea and slab of cake I was carrying. "You don't like iced tea and chocolate goodness?" Disbelief had me raising my brows. "Did something else happen when that vamp kicked your arse? Did the steel cut through some sort of good-taste artery, or are you just being a stubborn idiot who can't simply be looked after for one night?"

There was no doubt Thatch made the worst patient ever. It was the same day and we were already home, Thatch on at least one night's bed rest before he should be healed and back to it tomorrow, and me on strict instructions from the doctor to make him do just that. But bloody hell, Thatch would barely sit still, let alone take help with grace.

"That vamp was pumped up to the eyeballs with something."

"I'd have thought it was the other way around, since his foot was up your arse." I promptly moved out of the way as he threw the TV remote in my direction. It clattered to the floor and miraculously didn't break.

"You're so lucky that's still intact. How would you watch your shit shows without it?" I was prodding a bull, but him being like this had got my mouth firing nineteen to the dozen. I figured it was my reaction to him being well, and the sarcasm and jibes my way of coping with how close I had come to losing him.

"Fine. The drink and cake are great. Thanks." Every word was forced. In response, I gave him the stink eye but handed over the goods regardless. He took a bite of the rich chocolate and sighed happily. Pleasure thrummed through me. He was safe and no longer in danger. Plus he now had cake, so I could eat my slice and relax a little.

"Have you heard anything about the girls?" he asked after finishing a mouthful.

I nodded, cake still in my mouth. After swallowing and taking a drink, I said, "Yeah, Meadows called a couple of hours ago when you were sleeping. Said they were being well taken care of. They're still running tests on Carly, the girl who we saved last. They're anticipating her being okay and are working on the premise that the piece-of-crap doc was still in the process of drawing blood rather than pumping who knows what inside her."

When Meadows had been the one to call me, taking me by surprise that he'd been able to get my number, I'd been relieved to hear the news. Having the girls taken was too close to comfort. Too close to Lucinda.

"That's great news. Will SICB keep us updated?"

"Yeah." I nodded. "Meadows said his sister is part of

the medical team working her case. As soon as he has anything, he'll give me a call."

A frown formed on Thatch's face. His deep brown eyes penetrated mine, almost making the flecks of green not visible in his intensity.

"What?" I shifted to face him, worry flaring to life.

"Meadows. Why's he letting you know?"

Huh. I tilted my head, trying to get a read on Thatch. After a beat, I grinned.

"What?" He all but growled the word.

"Meadows asked me if he could call me some time." I left the statement hanging there. The grin on my face couldn't grow any wider once a full-on growl erupted from him. Not quite so cruel to keep him hanging, despite my obvious pleasure, I said, "Calm down there, big guy. I said I wasn't interested."

Who'd have thought a huffing man doing a crappy job at pretending to be unaffected could be so hot? Wrap that same guy in a package of dry wit and a take-charge attitude, and hot could easily become molten.

His huff turned into a sigh, and he took a large bite of his cake. Ignoring his reaction, he then asked, "And what about the doctor we were able to apprehend?"

There was no chance I could keep Thatch from talking about the case, not that I necessarily wanted him to. He wasn't made that way, even when healing.

"They've got her in holding. Her name's Dr Sarah Benedict. She gave a fair amount of intel without too much persuasion. Kent's gathering a few leads to see how much truth there is in what she's given." I eased back on the sofa and finished off my drink. "The vamp who kicked your arse was on Vesper, a new drug this organisation has been apparently trialling. Heard of it?" Kent hadn't mentioned any knowledge of it when asked, and I never had. Though, I assumed it had some relation to the original drug I was tracking down when I first stumbled into Thatch's investigation, as well as his life, which I'd be sure to confirm when I got the chance.

"No." Thatch shook his head and put down his empty plate. "What's it do?"

"Exactly what you thought. Ramps up a vamp's powers but for a limited time, according to Doc Evil."

A quirked brow was Thatch's response.

I grinned. At least I entertained myself, a necessary distraction when the shit was hitting the fan. "It's not in mass production yet, and she'll give the production lab to us if we grant her a safe haven from the powers that be."

He quirked both brows this time. I reacted in kind.

"Yeah. Surprised me too, but if your previous assessment was right and the organisation is indeed floundering, she's securing her position now rather than going down with the ship."

"And any idea who the lead player is yet?" he asked.

"Nope. And she's refusing to give a name. Says giving the drugs up won't kill her, but names definitely would." Me? I wasn't so convinced about that. The operation seemed as vast as it did deadly. The doc giving up something as lucrative and as potent as Vesper and us stopping it before it got out on the street seemed like a big hit to me.

If she made it alive to the supe courts, I'd be surprised. And honestly, I wouldn't lose a bit of sleep should she be taken out. Unless it was on my watch, of course.

"Has she shed any more light on why female shifters specifically?" Tension thrummed through him as he asked the question.

"Yeah." I bobbed my head and exhaled before answering, my mood shifting as I recalled all Kent had told me. "It seems the manipulation of female shifter blood is the key to making the drug... this Vesper... less temperamental. Something in the chromosome assists with the stability. Has the potential to stop vamps losing their shit quite so quickly, while ramping up their existing senses." When Kent had passed on the info, the knowledge had done nothing to lessen the horror of all that had transpired.

Experimenting on women, *children* for the production of a drug.... Just the thought swelled my anger, encouraging me to turn and seek out Doc Evil to make her pay. Thatch's soft voice tugged me to him.

"And that's why they were also trying to create shifters too. To create more blood for more experiments, and then more ingredients for drug production."

The calmness in his voice belied the horror of his words. But making sense of it all eased my anger a little. Getting the facts, knowing it all, gave us power. It meant we could stop this from happening.

A quick glance at the time told me it was just gone six. "You think you can try to shift?" I asked, clutching the distraction. Plus, Thatch needed to be at full health. Not only for himself but my sanity too. Doc Holland had recommended a shift late afternoon, followed by a gentle stretch of his legs. I'd snorted at that. Trying to rein in a shifter when in animal form was ludicrous, but her stern gaze had told me enough: if he hurt himself, I'd be responsible.

"Can do." He stood and stretched carefully, wincing slightly when his stomach pulled.

"I think we're better off walking to the dam and taking a swim." Logically it made sense. Paddling would be a better way to take it easy rather than me having to pounce on him to stop him running or biting his tail or something. I wasn't sure how he'd handle the latter, even though I'd find it really entertaining.

When he looked nonplussed, I explained my reasons—without the pouncing and biting.

"That makes sense."

Side by side, we walked the short distance to the dam. It was just turning dusk, with the sliver of moon already present but no stars yet out.

"How are you really feeling?" I asked, unsure if he'd answer truthfully or not, what with the bravado most of us in the agency carried, regardless of species or gender.

A few moments of silence followed before he answered. "Amazing, all things considered." He paused as he reached the edge of the dam and angled towards me but focussed on the sky when he said, "It's a bit hard to believe that a couple of months back in this same situation on the operation, I'd likely have been dead." His head dropped, his gaze roaming my face, and my heart clenched at the truth of his words.

"I keep going over what-ifs." He shook his head and exhaled. His voice was low, barely above a whisper, but crystal clear for my supernatural hearing. "If Hazel hadn't gifted me with her abilities, last night—"

"I get it." Or as much as I could since I was born a

shifter so hadn't known a human existence. "I can't imagine how crazy all of this has been on you. Sometimes I forget you weren't born this way," I admitted. Since the reality of his turning interlocked with my sister's death, it was undeniably the real reason I crammed that in the depths of my mind. It was safer for me there. "And...." I trailed off, hating the complexity of my feelings, hating the thoughts that barrelled into my head.

"And what?" he pushed.

Pressing my lips firmly together, I tempered my emotions as much as possible before admitting, "I'm relieved you're here. Happy as hell that you're a shifter and survived tonight." Sentiment threatened to clog my throat, but with no sarcasm bubbling to the surface, no witty deflection on my tongue, I either needed to shut the hell up and jump in the dam or admit what was plaguing me. I snorted humourlessly.

"What's wrong?" Thatch moved a fraction closer, his hand taking hold of my arm, giving a gentle squeeze that I worried would finally be my undoing.

"It's all levels of screwed up, right?" I shook my head and made eye contact with him. "Me celebrating you're a shifter and grateful for the fact. What's that say about me, when the reason why you're all those things is because my sister's dead?" I didn't breathe, couldn't if I tried. The slightest of movements, reactions, and I could so easily fall apart.

When Thatch's large hand clamped around my neck and his forehead touched mine, I gasped, inhaling deeply, luxuriating in the cooler evening air filling my lungs that tasted of Thatch. We stood in silence. Me breathing, and Thatch showing me the way with his controlled inhales and exhales.

A few minutes passed, though it could have been a lot longer considering the calm infusing my limbs. I felt heavy, wrung out. So bloody tired of it all.

"I'm sorry" tumbled out of my mouth. "You were seriously injured, and I'm meant to be the one looking after you. Instead, I'm here being fu—"

While his movement was fast, so incredibly so that it took me by surprise, his mouth on mine was soft. Thatch worked my lips with his, pressing against them, encouraging me to open for him. A flick of his tongue against the seam of my mouth had me groaning and heat licking up my spine.

Reacting to his mirrored groan, I threaded my hands through his short crop of hair. The sweetness disappeared. In its place, desire sprung to life.

The fear of finding him. The fear of losing him. My guilt. The pull he had over me since that moment in Crandore. Every single moment had led to this moment.

Thank Christ any last scrap of resistance between the two of us shattered.

Dragging me closer to him, his hands worked my jeans. I took action immediately, my mission to shed his clothes something I was totally on board with. A guttural moan rent the air when his hand clamped around my bare flesh. Impatient for more, I broke the kiss and tugged his shirt off, mine quickly following. Our eyes locked. Unsure what to expect, relief eased through me when his lips pulled into a smile. As I tugged his pants down a little, my eyes drifted to where I took him in my hand. His dark skin was silky smooth and so hot I was sure there'd be scorch marks in my palm. I swiped up and down, my eyes never breaking from his, and through sheer will alone, I managed not to close my eyes when he pumped my length. His hand was big and rough, with the perfect firmness. There was no way I would last.

"Fuck," I said on a groan, my hand not stopping jerking him off. "You're meant to be taking it easy." The barest of laughs rushed out my mouth just as my stomach clenched as he continued to caress me.

"I am," he whispered, following up with a sweet kiss that was nothing like the pace he used to jerk me off. Pulling his mouth away, a small smile curved his lips. I took that as my cue to twist a little and reach close to his groin to flutter my fingers over his balls. His wide-eyed response had me returning his grin before my muscles tightened and heat gathered, this time in the base of my spine.

"You are?" I managed to say.

"Yeah," he said breathily. "It's why you're in my hand and not me."

His words were too much. The heat turned into flames racing across my body. I had no choice but to slam my eyes closed and press my head against his shoulder as I exploded. My grip tightened on him, somehow remembering to keep working him and not stop or squeeze his cock off as my release tore through me.

Just as he was easing off me, his hand tightened and he coated my hand. His soft moan accompanied his release, the sound something I captured and held on to.

Slowing down my movements, both our bodies still tense and shuddering, my eyes opened fully. Not willing to let go of him and break the moment just yet, I leaned forward, pressing my lips to his. Our mouths teased each other's, and I smiled against his lips, crazy pleased he kissed me back so willingly.

"Swim in the dam and then a shift?" I suggested as I angled away from him.

"Yeah." His eyes searched mine. Unsure what he was

looking for, I withdrew my hand and followed up with a peck on the lips.

"Come on then. Get your tired arse in there." I stripped off my jeans fully and made my way to the bank, wading in before Thatch reached me. It didn't take him long before he was naked at my side. I glanced over at him. "Still holding up?" I asked, concern lilting my voice.

There went that eye-roll again, but this time with a gentle "Yeah. I'm good."

CHAPTER 8

COMPLICATED WASN'T QUITE THE RIGHT WORD for it. And I wasn't talking about the handjob I'd given Thatch. Instead, it was the whole-unit-being-practically-off-the-books thing, ensuring the "right" details were disclosed to the appropriate people.

I supposed my subterfuge was easy enough, since I was a known agent in Brent's team. So there were no name changes, not that much deception beyond that I'd been reassigned to a small division for a sting operation.

The problem lay with Thatch and ensuring the titles, his role, the details assigned to his position fit. I'd already had to evade Lucas's questions a few too many times and was having to do it again now. This time with Thatch by my side.

"Bloody hell, look what the cat dragged in." Lucas

stood and gave me an unceremonious hug. "Was beginning to think you'd pissed Brent off so much he'd finally dug a hole for you."

I snorted as I patted his back. "As if." I stepped out of his embrace and glanced at Thatch, who remained stoic at my rear. It was obvious he didn't like the familiar contact between me and Lucas from the gritting of his teeth. It was heady, him reacting that way. A guy could certainly get used to it. "Thatch, Lucas."

At the mention of Lucas's name, understanding seemed to register and Thatch's jaw unclenched. I'd shared enough about my life for Thatch to know who Lucas was. He stepped forward and held out his hand for Lucas to shake. Lucas did so immediately, but I didn't miss the slight inclination of his head as he cast me a look that meant he figured I had the hots for Thatch.

The guy had a weird ability to read me so clearly. Whether body language, scent, or he simply knew my type so well, I did not want to get into this with him. And definitely not since we were at the main offices for Brent's division.

I cast Lucas a pointed look as he stepped away from Thatch and sidled close to him. The arsehole quirked his brow at me in challenge.

"Later." I groaned in defeat and glanced at Thatch, who appeared bemused.

Before I had the chance to say anything else, Brent stepped out of his office. "Thatcher," he said, and reached out to shake his hand. "Let's head to the conference room." He turned his back on me without any acknowledgement. He was such a turd.

Refusing to let him affect me, I rolled my eyes at Lucas, then stepped next to Thatch and headed to Brent, who turned at the door to open it. His gaze landed on me, and I was certain he was desperate to sneer but seemed to be holding himself in check.

"Callen, you can wa—"

"Callen's in the meeting with me." Thatch's response was immediate.

I clamped on to the insides of my cheeks to stop the grin trying to form.

"But I don't—" Brent attempted, but Thatch cut him off.

"It's not open for discussion."

Thatch was so getting my tongue in his mouth as soon as we were in the car. Stolen kisses filled the past few days, as well as an ease that had taken us by surprise. We hadn't truly got hot and heavy yet, beyond that first time by the dam and the fantastic hand action. With late nights and us stepping up the investigation based on the intel Doc Evil gave us, it meant little time for much else. But I'd make it a point to get him hot and heavy as soon as possible.

Without another word, Brent entered the room, the two of us following close behind. I sat, Thatch taking the seat next to me, while Brent took the chair opposite.

Despite Brent being the one who asked to see Thatch regarding Crandore Laboratories, Thatch said, "What have you got on Crandore Laboratories that wasn't on file or couldn't have been sent over secure transfer?"

And my hard-on for the man by my side reached new levels of uncomfortable. Calling Brent out on his BS was heady as hell.

Discomfort had Brent's brows furrowing, followed by his left eye twitching, meaning he was pissed off. That same tell had been directed my way too many times to count in the three years I'd managed to stay in his team. I still marvelled how I'd lasted so long. Breaking the rules, and all but telling Brent where to go on a semi-regular basis had been my norm. The reasons behind him keeping me on confused me something rotten. Yeah, I was a good agent and got the job done, but he could have easily palmed me off to a different area. Yet he hadn't.

I squashed those thoughts, needing to stay focussed

on whatever Brent was about to say. I just wondered if he'd be ballsy enough to be an arsehole to Thatch or not.

"I'm sorry to have inconvenienced you…" Apparently his balls had shrivelled and disappeared. I swallowed my snort as Brent continued. "…but I thought it was important to touch base on your investigation."

I stilled at that, waiting to see how Thatch would respond.

"And what investigation is that?"

Considering the confidentiality surrounding Thatch's team, I had to wonder what Brent was hoping to achieve by bringing Thatch here and attempting to question him. And more to the point, why had Thatch agreed to come along in the first place?

My eyes widened when Brent's cheeks flushed. It didn't take long for him to steady himself, but his discomfort piqued my interest.

"Crandore Laboratories and Jonas Cartwright—"

"What about Jonas Cartwright?" Thatch's voice didn't lilt, didn't change in pitch, giving nothing away. We both knew no one outside of our team and the director—including her top security team who'd taken Cartwright from our hands—should be aware we'd manage to capture him in the first place.

Brent blanched. His eyes darted away before

returning to Thatch. "Have you been able to secure his location yet?"

Remaining mute, Thatch stared at him hard.

My gaze flicked between the two of them, the silence deafening.

"I mean—" Brent cleared his throat. "—we've just pulled in a shipment of LIXER, and with you investigating—"

Without inflection, Thatch asked, "Who said we were investigating Jonas Cartwright or LIXER?"

The eye twitch worked its way to the rest of Brent's face. "It doesn't take a genius to know you're investigating them, since that's where you were almost killed and turned into a dirty mutt."

Wide-eyed, I planted my feet firmly to the ground. The urge to pounce on him thrummed through me. Brent was human, so any slight nick of my claws could kill the arsehole. While struggling to dispel the anger working its way through me, I would never allow this tosser to be the reason why I destroyed my career, or quite possibly my life.

From the corner of my eye, the slightest shift in heat coming from Thatch caught my attention. Boy, was he pissed. He stood, and I followed suit, careful to stay close in case I needed to intervene. I'd had three years of dealing with Brent's slurs, though they tended to refer to the scum of my father and the embarrassment of my family name. It seemed his contempt went a whole lot deeper than the Blackheath name and stretched as wide as all shifters. Whether that was just wolves or the species at large, who knew.

I wished I could say I didn't care, but as a SICB division manager, his power and hatred were not a combination that put me at ease.

"I think perhaps we've finished here," Thatch said, his rage obvious.

Scrambling from his chair, Brent flushed. "I'm not sure—"

With a sharp turn away from the door and back to Brent, Thatch peered down at him. The air rippled around him, all contained anger and contempt. Shock registered on Brent and he took a step back before he seemed to realise what he'd done and stood straighter. "Let me be clear, Brent, there is nothing you need to know about anything my team or I do. And if I find you sniffing around, I'll pull a wall of hurt down on you so fast you won't know your arsehole from your elbow." He waited a beat, and from the flicker of Brent's gaze from me to Thatch, I assumed he was allowing the threat to sink in. Thatch then turned.

I angled out the way so he could reach the door first, a flurry of pride for Thatch laying it out there balancing for a hold on my anger at Brent for being a prejudiced prick.

Hand to the door, Thatch angled his head over his shoulder. "Don't let me hear you refer to shifters as mutts again. Your time at the SICB will be an awfully difficult place to be if Durrant gets a whiff of it." He grasped the handle, opened the door, and we both headed out.

Surprising even myself that I'd kept my mouth shut, I kept walking in silence towards the office exit, throwing a concerned Lucas a wink and a chin lift on my way out. This was Thatch's fight. While I'd be there every step of the way, his rank alone meant I'd needed to let him handle it all.

As soon as we hit the open air, I mumbled, "You know that was all kinds of hot, right?"

He snorted, his reaction making me smile and relaxing my tense shoulders.

"Is that right?"

"Yep. If we weren't in this car park right now, I'd totally be sucking your..." I glanced at him, offering him a smirk. "...tongue."

His laugh was loud and infectious. It lit my stomach and made warmth dance in my chest. "Probably best to wait till later." He cut his eyes to me as we reached his car.

I grinned widely. "I promised myself earlier that I'd wait till we were in the car." And that was pushing it. I was hot for the guy. Big time. And while I constantly warred with myself about him being a distraction to me, and vice versa, and that we should wait... blah blah blah... that was exactly how my internal discussion went. I zoned myself out, telling myself to get over it.

Perhaps not the sagest of advice, but I convinced myself that sometimes my rash decisions paid off. Plus, how rash really was this thing between us?

Thatch pulled his sunglasses on and shook his head at me. I was sure he was also surveying the area to see if I could follow through with minimum risk. "Get your arse into the car."

I scrambled in as soon as the doors unlocked, keeping my belt off and facing him in expectation. As soon as he sat, I reached out and tugged his glasses off, needing to see the heat in his eyes.

I wasn't disappointed.

Our mouths met in a clash of tongues and groans. Both of us knew it couldn't last long. Urgency swept through me as our mouths pressed against each other's, moving together in perfect rhythm, like his mouth was made to connect with mine.

He broke away before I did. A protest threatened to fall out of my mouth when my eyes connected with his.

Immediately I clamped my mouth shut. Heat swirled in his gaze. In response, my lips lifted.

"What?" His question was low and breathy.

"You want me."

If he'd asked me that, I would have probably given a wise-arse remark. Instead, he simply said, "Yes."

My smile in place, I flicked my gaze to his before leaning in and pressing my mouth against his in a brief kiss. As I pulled away, I said, "That's good. It means I can keep coping with blue-ball kisses." I tugged the seat belt and locked it into place.

"Blue-ball kisses?" Amusement lifted his words.

"Yep. Blue-ball kisses. Every damn time, and that's okay." I gave a small one-shoulder shrug even though there was no hiding how affected I was. Not in the confined space and with our senses on high alert.

When he remained quiet and still hadn't started the engine, I peered over at him. He was studying me, his focus intense.

"What?" I asked.

"Just wondering if the blue balls pose more or less of a distraction."

I sighed, understanding his meaning completely. "Screwed if I know."

He tapped his fingers on the wheel, an unusual tell from Thatch who rarely gave anything away. *Unless he's with me.* The thought took me by surprise as I registered the truth of it.

"It's either 'let's just hold back until this nightmare case is put to rest and risk blue balls pushing us to such despair that we end up only thinking about burying our dicks into each other,' *or* 'screw all that, let's get down and dirty, potentially putting the both of us at risk as it means not only will we be *thinking* of what that feels like, but it means that we've taken this to the next level and could possibly put an innocent at risk to save the other?'" I gasped for air after spouting all that at him.

His eyes were wide, and I was sure I'd rendered him speechless until he said, "So you put some thought into this then?"

I gave a humourless laugh. "Only since the night we met."

For the barest of seconds, his mouth gaped before he clamped it shut.

"Right! Already it's eating into our time where we should be back working out our next move and what the hell Brent is playing at." The reality uncurled in my gut, leaving an unpleasant feeling in its wake. "I agree, it's shit and a bit of a catch-22 situation."

He sighed and rubbed his hand over his face. "I hate that you're right."

I appreciated his honesty. Didn't like it, but what

was a guy to do? The only alternative was to stop anything more from happening, and there was no way I was going to suggest that possibility. Call me a selfish dick, but yeah... I was a selfish dick. Swallowing back my frustration, I offered him a small smile. "We'll figure it out." My words came out more certain than I felt. "We'd best head back."

He nodded, strapped in, and pulled away.

The drive went by with us dissecting Brent's intent as well as discussing a file that Kent had found from the night we'd taken in Doc Evil, who we were relieved to discover was a major player. While the latter was a boon, it didn't mean that operations would close, not with the corrupt organisation having so many fingers in so many damn pies.

"I'm going to meet with Kent and discuss a few ways to keep tabs on your good friend," Thatch said as we entered the building.

I raised my brows at that. "Are you able to do that? Legally I mean?"

His grin was disarming, and it took all my strength not to do a happy sigh that it was directed at me. "One of the many wonderful things about flying under the radar is that we're not always expected to play by the rules. How our operation runs has always been very clear: we pass through the tape like the ghosts we are."

I rolled my eyes and headed to my desk as he called Kent into his office.

I'd barely sat my butt down when my phone rang. I sighed and dipped my hand into my back pocket.

After a quick glance, I answered with "Lucas."

"Thought you could escape without making good on those drinks you promised, huh?" His voice was tight.

A frown pulled my brows low. Lucas knew I didn't drink. Not only that, his tone was off. "Sure. You want to tell me where and what time?" Uneasiness floated in my insides, especially as it hadn't been that long since I'd seen him. I glanced at my watch. Probably forty minutes.

"The usual place."

I went on high alert. Lucas either suspected or knew his calls were being monitored. Or perhaps it was mine that were. The only "usual" place referred to an old warehouse he owned. One he kept off the books and I was sure fewer than three people knew about. It was security-proofed like crazy.

"Got it. Malones it is," I said, referring to a bar twenty minutes in the other direction. "What time works?"

"Just have a couple of things to do here. Should be good for maybe eight." Which meant an hour earlier.

"Sounds like a plan." I didn't give him a chance to

respond before I ended the call. Concern barrelled through me. My thoughts immediately went to Brent and our meeting. The whole thing had reeked of koala shit.

A glance across the room told me Thatch was still meeting with Kent. As if feeling my eyes on him, he lifted his head, his gaze fixing on me through the glass wall. His look was questioning, his brows dipping. He followed up with a head flick in his direction. Not needing a further invite, I hauled arse over there.

On entering, I sat in one of the empty chairs, and Kent continued speaking.

"There's no chance we can get into his phone. His laptop, maybe. But I imagine everything will be encrypted and in the cloud, so I'm unsure of our chances." Frustration ebbed off her. That was the difficulty when trying to focus on one of our own. Their technology and safeguards were the same as ours.

"We may not need to," I said, my gaze fully on Thatch.

His eyes bored into mine as he asked, "What have you got?"

"Lucas contacted me for a private meet."

Thatch's eyes widened at that.

"Mathew Lucas?" Kent asked.

"Yeah, know him?" While they were both vamps and

both in the same city, that didn't necessarily mean they were—

"He's my sister's ex."

The hell?

Frowning, I tried to think of any girlfriends Lucas had had since knowing me. Absolutely zero came to mind, which may have been bloody weird until I realised that I was in the same boat. Penises had come and gone for me, but I'd not wanted any of them to stick around.

My gaze travelled to Thatch. Yeah, until Thatch.

I shook that thought away and asked, "Girlfriend?"

The familiar roll of her eyes followed. "Before you were born, cub."

I scratched my nose with my middle finger. Her lips twitched, which was as good as saying she thought I was awesome. Meanwhile, Thatch exhaled a deep breath, drawing our attention to him. Wide-eyed and unimpressed, he waited for me to continue.

"I'm meeting him in a while. I have no specifics, but I can't help but think it's related to our meeting with Brent."

Thatch bobbed his head. "Where are you meeting him?"

Relief and warmth swirled in my chest when he didn't immediately demand an invite. Trust was a heady thing, and beyond Lucas, it had been a long time since

I'd had any thrown my way. Just like I didn't hand it out often.

I shook my head. "As soon as I have anything, I'll come home—"

Kent made a small noise in the back of her throat. Not sure if it was amusement or that she was thirsty or what, I stared at her hard until I realised what she was reacting to.

Despite the heat racing to my cheeks, I reined in my reaction, and rather than telling her to bugger off, I averted my gaze to Thatch and continued. "—and give you an update." Amusement shimmered in his eyes, alongside something else I couldn't get a read on. Perhaps he liked that I'd called his place home, though I was sure it wasn't the first time that faux pas had slipped out.

"Are we going to work theories or just wait to see what Lucas has for us?" I asked, determined to focus.

"I think we just wait and see what the meet is for. Kent's also been working on decrypting data we expect to be your Doc Evil's shopping list and formula to not only LIXER, but to whatever they're using to try to turn humans into shifters."

Which was also quite possibly connected to the experiments done on my sister. The more we discovered about the operation and the links, which I'd spent hours poring over from the team notes they'd acquired over the past eighteen months or so, the more it became apparent that an antidote of some sort was needed.

For those who OD'd on LIXER and the selection of other drugs Thatch's team had found a connection to, all had died. No one had escaped the effects of the drugs or the experimentations. When Thatch had told me about the few individuals who'd managed to survive, it was only because they were at the end of the queue. Legit, the nasty bastards who ran the show simply hadn't got to them yet.

"That's good news," I answered.

"If we can at least get ourselves prepared to save anyone else who's impacted, then that has to be worth something till we nail the arseholes," Kent said.

"Agreed." I nodded. "I read the report out of SICB this morning that there's been a reduction in drug-related deaths."

"With our focus on closing production labs, we believe it's a direct correlation to them simply running out of production space and victims." Thatch's anger matched my own when he spoke. We all knew there was an increased chance of more shifters being taken. While chemicals were the base of the drugs, it was what they were being used for that was the problem.

With all the drugs and experimentations involving

blood, while the vampire community at large was the focus of the market, that didn't mean that a vamp was behind it. We'd be foolish to jump to conclusions.

At the moment, the issues were largely in the greater Sydney region, but we knew it wouldn't take long to spread. It was that we also needed to control.

We all turned and faced the door as Jenson appeared. He opened the door when Thatch indicated he should enter.

"You know that looked freaky weird, right? You all did this fast head turn at the exact same moment when I was about ten feet away from your door." He gave a mock shudder.

"Get your arse in here." Thatch's gaze settled on the paperwork in Jenson's hands. He reached out for it, and as he flicked through, he ordered, "Debrief."

"We have the warrants for the three supe clubs you wanted us to get. We have three SICB teams taking point on all of them. They'll be hit at the same time. Jamison is going to lead, and all reports are going back to him."

While I was already paying attention and was aware Thatch had wanted to focus on a few clubs, Jamison's name had me sitting up straighter. When I looked away from Jenson and at Thatch, his eyes were on me. I eased back a little, trying to appear unaffected, but only the human in our midst would be buying that.

"Did you ensure the specifics of it being a drug bust were given?" Thatch asked.

"Sure did. They're not looking for any drug specifically, nor has anyone been made aware we're behind the raid. As far as even Jamison is aware, orders are coming from vice and Detective Thatch Miller in a joint operation."

Thatch nodded, and I eased back even more at that as I spent too much time figuring out Jamison didn't even know Thatch's real name or role. A welcome heat filled me at the thought, right alongside my desire to sucker punch myself for focussing on what really didn't matter in the moment.

"Sounds good. Thanks. Anything else?" Thatch's focus returned to the paperwork in his hands.

"Nope, that's it for the moment."

Kent stood. "I'll walk you out. I want to go over something with you."

Jenson nodded, and I couldn't help but wonder why she never gave him shit like she did me.

"Call me when you get *home*, Callen, if you have something that requires my immediate attention. If not, I'll see you both in the morning." She flashed her teeth at me, and I closed my eyes in return, giving a soft shake of my head.

Before the door closed, I heard Jenson's question: "What was that about? Are they legit official now or—"

I tuned him out and squinted in Thatch's general direction. "So, I best get going."

When Thatch remained silent for a beat, I hesitated before finally standing, still unsure about his hard stare. It was common knowledge he could be a scary arsehole at the best of times, but throw in that intensity and I wasn't sure what exactly he was feeling or doing.

"All good?" I dared to ask, not quite sure if I wanted to know his answer. But I was rarely one to pussyfoot around a situation.

Remaining seated, he didn't shift, didn't twitch. The intensity ramped up a notch before he said, "I know you trust Lucas, and it's the only reason I'm allowing you to go this alone."

My brows sprang high, and I opened my mouth to challenge him, but he continued, quickly saying, "One, because I'm your boss and this is work-related, but also because if I thought you were in danger, there's no way I'd be letting you step out there alone." The slightest of pauses led him to say, "I just need you to get in, get what you need, stay safe, and come home to me. Got it?"

With my heart beating wildly, it was a struggle to hear myself think, and I wasn't quite sure of the volume of my voice when I said, "Because you like me." My shit-eating grin was all sass; it belied the flood of emotions raging through me at his words. *He really bloody likes me.* That knowledge alone was enough to make sure I got back to him safely. "Home" to him. I totally didn't miss that drop, whether teasing or not.

Thatch quirked his brow. "I said, got it?"

I nodded, my smile becoming less of a grin and more of "I really wish I could kiss your face off right now." So not appropriate in his office. "Thanks for trusting me to know my friend."

"From what you've told me, he's been the only one for the past twelve years who's had your back."

I didn't need to respond to that since he spoke the truth.

"That means I'll put my faith in you, but you need to know you can trust me too."

My response was immediate and threaded with my truth. "I do. Completely. Shit, maybe more than anyone, and isn't that a mindfuck moment?"

Thatch pressed his lips together, which I didn't see him often do. He was holding something back.

"You best go before I hold on and can't let you walk out of here." His gaze was unwavering, the intensity still the same. And without a doubt, if I didn't hightail it out of there, I'd be throwing myself on his lap.

"Got it." I turned my back on him, my skin burning

up, so very aware of his gaze following me. After opening the door and turning to shut it, I said, "Steak sounds good." I threw him a wink and made my way to my desk, all too aware what lay between Thatch and me wouldn't be going away and couldn't remain undiscussed.

After I met with Lucas, it was time to lay our cards on the table.

CHAPTER 9

I'd checked to ensure I didn't have a tail and had looped around one of seven different routes here. Lucas was nothing if not a stickler for keeping his safehouse exactly that. Even if it was a huge warehouse used for working rather than a homey place to crash.

I had a unique code and even a retina scan to get in. It was extreme, but I figured considering his time on this earth, he'd picked up a heap of knowledge and skills. Plus, he regularly geeked out with technology, so it all made sense.

I headed straight through to the secondary secure room. Apparently this was where all the magic happened —completely Lucas's words. He was at the main panel, kitted out with a crazy number of screens. Some were linked to cameras around this place, a couple focussing on his base's entry points. He also had a screen up indicating a guy called Lentwood—a name and face I wasn't familiar with.

"All good?" I asked in the way of greeting.

"Let's have a conversation, then perhaps rephrase your question."

Crap. "Like that, huh?"

"Worse."

Double crap. "Okay, hit me." I pulled a chair out and sat off to his side. He swivelled and faced me.

He looked pale, more so than usual. His pale skin wasn't a result of his vampirism, rather his Scottish roots. Not only that, he appeared exhausted. How was such a noticeable difference possible since I'd seen him just a few hours ago?

Rather than asking, I kept my mouth shut and waited for him to speak.

"I've been digging for a while."

I raised my brows at that. Even though I had no idea into what, I wasn't surprised. Lucas was the king of research and uncovering shit people would rather you left alone. He was also something of a conspiracy theorist, which sometimes made life interesting, but he'd research the hell out of something to either confirm or deny.

"Brent's dirty."

I froze. This was serious.

"I've always kept tabs on him, just because he's an arsehole." I snorted at that, and he offered a small smile before saying, "But since you left to join the ITU—"

My brows lifted high and my heart went a little crazy.

He shook his head and rolled his eyes at me. "As if I wouldn't know about the ITU. Come on, give me some credit."

I laughed. "Okay, and thank fuck for that, as it was bullshit not being straight with you."

"I get it, but this is me. You should have figured I'd find out."

True that. I indicated for him to go on; I was listening despite the loud beat of my heart trying to make that task difficult.

"Brent's been on a big anti-Callen trip, more than usual. Not only that, but he's been trying to access a restricted database, which I've discovered only two people have access to."

"Thatch and Durrant?"

"You've got it."

"Do you know just how far his dirt spreads?"

"I'm still digging, but shit... you're not going to like this."

Dread threatened to drop my gut. I steeled myself, wondering where he was going with this.

"There's been an increase in shifter disappearances."

"The girls?"

Lucas shook his head. "I heard about them, but no, that's not what I'm referring to. Shifters from up north."

I stilled at that. "As in far north."

My father's pack, my old home.

"I've found communication between Brent and the Blackheath pack."

"Fuck." I swallowed hard, unsure how to feel. "Between my dad? About what? When?" I fired at him.

He waited patiently for me to refocus before he said, "Yes, with Lennon Blackheath. There's been communication for at least five weeks, but that doesn't mean it hasn't been going on for longer. From what I can tell, it's about the missing shifters."

I grimaced. "And I can assume it's not because my father's been worried about shifter disappearances so has been helping the SICB?"

A barely perceptible shake of Lucas's head prompted him to say, "Have you heard of any shifter disappearances from up north?"

"No." My gut constricted. "Why haven't we?"

"It's all been completely off the radar. I'd be impressed as hell that something of this magnitude was able to be kept quiet if I wasn't sick to my stomach."

After focusing on my breathing while trying to get my thoughts together, I asked, "Just women and girls?"

"Only for the past month or so from what I can tell."

"No doubt thanks to the discovery of what they did to Hazel." Red-hot fury tinged with a desire to tear through not only Brent, but also my old pack for answers rode me hard. Lucas's words cut through my haze.

"What? What about Hazel?"

Bowing my head, I knew I needed to tell him everything. Screw protocol. This was all too messed up. Yes, Lucas knew she was dead, murdered, and considering the nature of her death and her body's location, a lot could be deduced. But official reports were not the truth.

My thoughts roamed to Thatch. I needed him here.

"You mind if I call Thatch and bring him in?" I understood what I was asking. And perhaps I was wrong, but this thing with Brent, let alone my father, was bigger than the two of us.

"You trust him."

Lucas's statement had me bobbing my head.

His eyes connected with mine, intense and curious. "And... you love him."

My eyes sprang open so damn wide, Lucas's snort of laughter made sense. After a moment of me gaping at him while trying to navigate through the impact of his words and whether or not my feelings went beyond lust and like, I settled on, "I have no idea how to answer that."

Amused, he shook his head at me. "Well, hopefully when you do answer it, you won't look quite as surprised as you do now." His grin was wide. "Holy shit, you haven't had sex yet!"

How the hell did he know that?

"Sex has always just been sex, right?"

I rolled my eyes, knowing he was absolutely right. I loved sex as much as every other guy, but Thatch and I hadn't taken that next step. It was a first for me, and I knew exactly the reason why.

"You think there's a deeper bond between the two of you?" He tilted his head in curiosity.

"Yeah, maybe." Okay, absolutely. Sex was simple and amazing, always. But sometimes between shifters, if the connection was strong, it moved things to a level of intensity I knew neither of us was ready for. We couldn't be. Not with our current mission.

Rather than Lucas winding me up further, I was relieved when he said, "And yes. Agree to meet him out at Valley Park and bring him here."

I sent a quick text to Thatch. He responded immediately, saying he'd meet me there in forty-five minutes. That gave me twenty-five minutes to share with Lucas everything about my sister, the case, and everything Thatch had been working on over the past two years. There was a connection somewhere. It was just that the introduction of Brent and Lennon bloody Blackheath was a development I never expected.

FOR FIVE HOURS WE'D BEEN LOOKING AT ALL the intel Lucas could provide, while Thatch caught him up with more in-depth details I hadn't gone into.

It was well past midnight, and I stifled a yawn, almost seeing double from staring at the screen in front of me.

When Thatch's firm grip latched onto my shoulders, I exhaled and angled my neck to look at him. "Hey." My smile was real, if sleepy.

"I think we should head out of here and recharge. I want to talk to Kent in the morning."

Lucas's grumbles reached us at the mention of Kent's name, and I laughed. In the bare-minimum break we'd taken between discussion, research, and trying to connect the dots, his link to Kent and her sister had given me the break I needed. It was always fun to take the piss out of the guy, and despite his conspiracy theories and his penchant for all things tech, there'd been little I'd been able to throw at him until now.

"That sounds like a plan." Since we weren't officially at work, I turned my head and kissed Thatch's arm, allowing a deep inhale of his skin. It was hard not getting handsy whenever the desire to touch him, scent him grabbed me, which was a lot. It was an aspect I struggled with. Maybe when I'd finally taken him, and him me, the struggle would ease off a little.

My dick twinged at the thought, and if I wasn't so tired, I'd be eagerly dragging him home and putting my mouth on him.

"Really?" Lucas's amusement split the air.

"What?" I didn't even try for innocence. "I can't help it. Will you just look at the man? He's hot as hell!" I wriggled my brows for good measure.

Lucas gagged, while Thatch snorted and hauled my arse out of the chair.

"I think that's our cue to leave," he said, sending Lucas an apologetic smile and then me a heated glance. Warmth uncurled in my stomach at the promise I saw there, which was immediately counteracted by my huge yawn that followed.

Lucas stood, following us towards the exit, laughing. "The only thing your arse is getting tonight is in bed."

I flicked him my middle finger. "Spin it, dude."

He snorted. "Yeah right, *dude!*" he mimicked. "I'll touch base with you tomorrow."

"I'll call you by 0900," Thatch said, focussing on Lucas. "That'll give me a chance to touch base with Kent." He paused before saying, "Are you sure it's okay to bring her here?"

My heart gave an extra beat at his thoughtfulness. It didn't take a lot to work out how off the grid Lucas's place was, and it mattered he was respectful of that.

"Yes, that's fine," he agreed, and by his quick acceptance, I couldn't help but wonder how many other secret lairs he had dotted around the country.

After saying goodbye, Thatch and I headed out, stopping to pick up his car on the way.

We were both hungry, but our exhaustion won out, so we tumbled into bed as soon as we were home, my limbs wrapping around Thatch's hot body.

It seemed like I'd only closed my eyes before I heard voices. It was Thatch on the phone. It would have been easy to zero in and figure out who he was talking to, one of the many lines a shifter—those with a healthy dose of respect—worked hard at not crossing, unless we were welcome to listen. Instead, I pried my eyes open and looked at the time on the nightstand. It was just gone six in the morning, which meant I'd managed to get four hours, if that.

When Thatch said goodbye to whoever was at the end of the line, he headed back to his room. His tall, well-defined form filled up the door frame. The sight of him was something I didn't think I could tire of looking at. He really was as close to perfection anyone could be. I hoped if this continued between us, he'd remain all mine.

"What's going on in that head of yours?" Thatch asked, leaning against the frame as his eyes raked me. I shifted a little, allowing the sheets to move to give him a glimpse of the trail that would one day very soon lead him to call out my name.

He quirked his brow at my movement, and I grinned. "You really want to know?" I asked.

His mouth twisted a little before he glanced at the clock. From his disappointed frown, I figured either way we didn't have time. "Rain check?"

"For what? Knowing what I was thinking?"

Pressing his lips together a beat, he finally said, "Yeah, let's stick with that."

Knowing we had shit to do and that neither of us was going to get any action, nor was there a chance of having that conversation that really needed to be had, I swung my legs over the edge of the bed, amusement beating through me when he groaned at my naked body.

"You're really not helping," he grumbled.

"I'm making this har—"

"Don't even."

I laughed when he stepped towards me, planting a fast kiss to my lips, and then backed out of his room quickly.

"You've got ten minutes. You can have your coffee on the way."

"Fine," I mumbled, equally as impressed as I was frustrated that he was a stickler at getting his job done.

Fifteen minutes later, much to my amusement at Thatch's grumbling, I was inhaling my black coffee on the way to headquarters.

"I'd best get you up to speed." He cast me a glance before saying, "Kent came round a couple of hours ago so we could talk without ears."

Surprise flittered through me. "How did I not hear that?"

A quirked brow followed by "Your snores were loud" was my answer.

"I would say I don't snore, but you'd only call bull-shit." But damn, I must have been really out of it to miss all that. I took a closer look at Thatch, wondering how he coped with what I assumed were just a couple of hours sleep. "How do you look so hot still, even with bags under your eyes?" My jest wrapped in truth.

"Hot comes naturally to me," he threw back, making me snort. "And obviously I have great genes."

I grinned, still taken by surprise when he joked around like this. It was also rare for him to talk about his family, however loosely. Aware it was a sensitive topic, I didn't bite. "So what'd Kent have to say?"

"She's organised a reconnaissance team to head to Blackheath territory. They should be there by midday. She's also managed to set up a drone to follow Brent's movements and planted bugs in his home office and car."

I wasn't even going to question how she managed that or whether or not they were secure. I'd learned not to doubt Kent's skill set. She didn't do half-arsed, period.

"All off the books?"

He nodded the affirmative. "I had a few favours I could pull."

"To be clear," I said, "are we expecting the link between Blackheath, Brent, and this Lentwood guy to be related to our investigation?" A ball of dread bounced in my gut as I waited for his confirmation.

"Yes."

I looked over at him, relieved when I didn't see pity aimed my way. "Thought so. I just don't understand the connection. Why would Brent get into bed with Blackheath? Not only does the arsehole hate shifters, but my old pack is hardly incognito." It was true. The pack had a reputation for violence and abuse of its pack members. They were also into arms dealing. It was that reputation that had made my life hell, not only when growing up in the pack, but when I'd joined the SICB. It took years for anyone to trust me. Except for Mathew Lucas.

"Blackheath was caught up in trafficking about three years ago, but nothing would stick."

"What?" I shook my head, this information being news to me.

"It was a sealed investigation."

I sighed. "So if we're thinking Brent is tied up with the missing shifters, the experiments, the blood farms, and what, the drugs as well, he's using Blackheath to kidnap more shifters?" The tangled mess of connecting cases threatened to blow my mind. "Where does Lentwood fit in?"

"Kent's working on leads based on what Lucas provided." He indicated to pull into our building. "We're collecting Kent and will be heading to Lucas's warehouse to work."

"What about the rest of the team?"

Thatch shook his head, his face turning hard. "I need them to continue running point on the intel Doc Evil provided. It's enough that the three of us are going to be AWOL. I can't have everyone in at this point. Not with Brent already trying to access data." He pulled up, engine still running when he said, "They'll know we're working on something I can't let them in on."

"And they'll be okay with that?"

Thatch turned to me, his dark brows raised high, a smirk aimed at me. "It's like you don't know me at all."

"Wisearse."

Seriousness filled his voice, belying the small smirk. "My team trust me to have their back and do what needs to be done."

I nodded, aware he spoke the truth. I just hoped he'd never have to be in a position to hold back from me. I got that it was his job, but withholding truths was shit. I supposed I'd have to cross that bridge if and when I came to it.

***

"I'm a genius!" Kent raised both hands high, a look of complete self-appreciation on her face. Her fingers moved quickly over her keyboard and she indicated towards one of the screens on the wall. "Xavier Lentwood, vampire, ex-militant originally from Michigan, USA. Suspected age over two hundred years. Last known residence Edinburgh, Scotland. Has lived under multiple aliases."

I took in the multiple images Kent had been able to

locate. Lentwood looked to be in his early thirties. His eyes were a dark grey that no doubt turned almost black when feeding.

"What else?" Thatch asked, knowing as much as I did that she'd have more on him.

"The last image we have of him is via CCTV footage in Melbourne eight days ago."

"And links to LIXER or the blood farms?" Thatch asked, taking a seat at the large table Kent and I occupied.

Lucas cleared his throat, a completely unnecessary action for a vampire that always amused me. But Lucas had been like that since I'd known him—portraying humanlike characteristics that were part of the training, used specifically to help humans feel more at ease.

We all looked in his direction when he said, "Seventy years ago, he had charges dropped that linked him to a vampire leisure drug called..." He glanced at the screen in his hand before continuing. "Bloodwhizz."

I snorted, loud and hard. "For real. Bloodwhizz? Holy shit." My laugh escaped, and I received a disapproving shake of the head from Thatch. I shrugged. "How can you not think that is ridiculously funny?"

Kent ignored me, saying, "I remember that. It was used as a relaxant and intended to enhance pleasure when feeding." I scrunched up my nose and received a middle finger from Kent. "It also was highly addictive and took SICB almost three years to get off the street and completely out of circulation. Sent its users into some sort of frenzy during their withdrawal."

"Frenzy?" I asked, immediately thinking of the vampire who had attacked Thatch.

"Yes," Lucas answered. "Something akin to a psychotic breakdown with a desperate thirst that addicts found unable to quench."

I winced. "Damn. It must have been a nightmare."

"It was," Kent said, her voice strangely neutral. "Thousands of humans and shifters were killed when it was on the streets, and addicted vampires had to be eliminated."

Wide-eyed, I stared at her, wondering why I'd never heard about this drug before.

"I recall the case," Thatch said, his brows scrunching and creasing his forehead.

"How? I've never heard of it." My eyes connected with his.

"You don't have security clearance. It was one of several cases over the history of the SICB that they pulled from the main records. After such a catastrophe, there was the fear that someone would try to replicate the drug, though not necessarily for its intended purpose."

"Are you thinking terrorism?" All too clearly, I could

see how effective a drug like that could be at sending vampires into a drug-fuelled frenzy to the point they could wipe out whole towns or cities. The idea chilled my veins.

"Yes." Thatch nodded solemnly. "I hadn't realised it was Lentwood linked to the drug. I don't recall all the details. How did he get off?"

Kent navigated to a different page. "A vampire called Timothy Garrison ended up taking the fall and cleared Lentwood's name."

"Do we have a link between Brent and Lentwood?" Thatch asked, his gaze travelling to Kent and Lucas.

Lucas shook his head while Kent backed it up with "No. But give us time."

Thatch nodded in response and looked at the time. I followed suit and saw it was midday. He pulled his phone out of his pocket and keyed in a number before placing it on the table and putting it on loudspeaker. "You're on loudspeaker," he said in greeting. "You in position?" His deep voice rumbled through the room, and goosebumps broke out across my skin immediately. Of course, both of the bloody vampires in the room noticed and sent me a smirk—Kent's teamed with her fingers in an L-shape on her forehead.

I simply shrugged. I didn't give a rat's arse that they knew how much he affected me.

"That is an affirmative."

I straightened at the voice. Bloody Jamison. He was everywhere it seemed, doing all sorts of favours for Thatch.

"What the—" I jolted back at the hard kick at my shin.

Kent gestured in my direction, a mixture of amusement and disgust on her face. "You were growling. It's not a good look on anyone, especially a loved-up operative who's struggling to keep his dick in his pants."

Fuck. My eyes darted to Thatch, whose eyes were on me. While he didn't look exactly pissed off, he wasn't exactly amused either. The voice, however, coming through the line sounded exactly that. "You holding out on me, Thatch?"

I shut my emotions down fast, carefully blanking my facial expression. My dick needed to behave, and that possessive growl that didn't like Jamison one damn bit needed to back off. Stat. There was no chance I could be responsible for putting Thatch in any unprofessional position. The knowledge startled the hell out of me. I'd never before given a damn about causing a stir or saying my piece, but when it came to Thatch, apparently, I was willing to play by the rules.

"That'll be Callen," Thatch offered.

"Blackheath?" Curiosity was evident in the question,

though not the usual disgust. Interesting, considering Jamison's current location.

"The one and only." His gaze hitting mine, Thatch didn't seem quite as pissed anymore.

"Huh. Anyone else see the irony at play here?"

I managed to keep my mouth shut and ignored Kent's snort.

"Trying to fuck Blackheath senior over while you're fucking his so—"

"Enough." Thatch shook his head, and while his one-word response brooked no argument, there was no heat behind the words.

Jamison's response was loud laughter.

"Considering how loud and ridiculous you're being, I'm assuming you're not at location?" Thatch said.

Jamison's laughter died down. "Not yet. I have a couple shadowing Blackheath, who's out on the road at the moment. I'm on base and due to head over to pack lands in a few hours. Rogers called in saying Blackheath used a payphone in town, so I'm working on getting that tapped."

"Just keep me updated."

"Will do. And, Thatch, you may want to do something so Callen doesn't need to be so possessive. Not that the growling isn't h—" Thatch ended the call, his eyes shifting to the ceiling.

"My bad," I said into the quiet. I didn't try to contain my smirk. "And just so you know, I'm totally down for whatever Jamison was suggesting."

Kent gagged, Lucas groaned, and Thatch walked off, mumbling, "Give me fucking strength."

"Something I said?" I waggled my brows at Thatch's retreating form before getting back to my research and pulling the headset on when I received an alert saying there was movement in Brent's vehicle.

The recording of movement kicked in immediately. It did on the opening of the door. Not only did the sensor track location, but it also provided an audio recording. After ten minutes of listening to a dodgy radio station, the music switched off midsong when an incoming call came in.

"You're late," an accented voice said. "Is there something I need to know?"

"No," Brent spoke immediately, a tone I'd only heard once, when he was unsure of himself. "I have an operative out today, so it was necessary to reassign a task. Nothing I can't handle."

"Tell me who the operative is."

"Why? You don't need t—"

"That wasn't a question."

Brent hesitated a moment before saying, "Lucas."

I cast a steady glance at the man in question. We wore matching headsets, and his eyes were on me.

"Mathew Lucas, the vampire?"

"That's correct."

There was silence for a few beats before the voice continued. "He's friends with Callen Blackheath." Once again, it wasn't a question.

Brent scoffed. "Not sure that mutt has friends, but I suppose if he did, Lucas would be the closest thing to it."

My jaw clenched as my heart picked up speed. This line of conversation filled me with unease.

"And what reason did Lucas provide for missing work? This would be unusual, I assume?"

Brent cleared his throat. "Lucas often takes a day working from home. It's part of his agreement."

I breathed a little easier at that. Intended or not, Brent might have just saved all our arses.

"Listen, Lentwood." My eyes sprang open and I called out for Thatch, who'd been in another room on a call. He was by my side immediately as Brent continued to dig the hole he was in. "I'm another fifteen minutes out, but I'll be there. I think I have a lead on the daughter."

Ice froze my breath, paused my lungs, and held me still.

"I will have my man contact you." The sound of a

loudspeaker signalled in the background. "If the lead is good, I'll be pleased. How did you get it?"

A heavy breath filled the car space before he spoke the words I desperately hoped he wouldn't: "Blackheath himself. Blood really can be bought."

I was mildly aware of them finishing the conversation. But with the rush of blood pounding in my ears and nausea curling in my gut, it was difficult to think of anything but Lucinda.

"Callen, I need your phone." Thatch's hands landed on my arms. "Phone, Callen."

Blinking through the haze, I struggled to focus, barely managing to reach in my pocket and hold it out, carelessly pressing my thumb over the ID scanner.

"Look at me." Firm, deep, and familiar, a voice I'd grown to trust implicitly cut through my spiralling fear. Once my eyes connected to his, I took a deep breath, finding reassurance in the green flecks amid the dark brown. "Take control and remember who you are and that this is what we do. Yeah?"

My nod was more controlled as I registered his words. I did not break under pressure. I would not fall in fear. And I absolutely would not let any bastard harm my niece. Certainty thrummed through me as I took control of my reaction, my emotions. Shoved every single errant thought away; they had no place with what had to be done.

"I'm good," I finally said, taking in the action around the room. There was an eerie focus in Kent and Lucas as they took immediate action in response to Brent's words. Even though I wasn't certain what they were actioning, without a doubt, it was to make sure Lucinda was safe.

Thatch's mouth connecting to mine took me by surprise. His warm lips pressed against my own, closed, pressure reassuring. I didn't even have time to respond beyond my wide-open eyes before he pulled back. Our faces close, I was able to take in the look he was giving me. I had no idea how so much could be said without words, but in that single gesture, that one look, the hulk of a man could easily make me fall to my knees from the reassurance he gave me.

"We won't let anything happen to Lucinda." Steel carried his words, brushing them across my lips as I allowed the truth of them to sink in.

"No, we won't."

Lips curving into a smile, he looked hotter than ever as he squeezed my neck and lifted my phone before hitting Call and placing it on the loudspeaker.

"Laketon" was offered in the way of greeting from the Blue Mountains alpha.

"Laketon, it's Liam Thatcher."

"Thatcher? Problem?" I appreciated Laketon cutting through formalities.

"Maybe. We need to get eyes on Lucinda—"

"I need to go to her," I said, cutting in. There was no way I could leave her protection in another's hands.

"Can you send us the coordinates to where she is?" Thatch asked immediately.

"What's going on? If there's a danger that may impact on my pack or the one who's keeping her safe, we need to know."

"There may be, yes. Send the coordinates over and we'll fill you in en route."

After Laketon begrudgingly agreed, I peered over at Thatch. Energy buzzed through me, willing to take charge and get me out of there so I could race ahead and make sure my niece was protected. It was Thatch's hard gaze telling me to keep my arse in place that kept me rooted, and the knowledge that half-cocked plans could potentially put Lucinda in more danger. It went against the core to hold back, but this was too important.

"Kent, talk to me." Thatch's gaze was still latched on to mine despite him addressing Kent.

"Chopper is ready in fifteen. You'll then need to shift to get to the coordinates Laketon sent. It's remote and only accessible by foot. The drop will be a town over from where Laketon's pack is. When he sent the details, he indicated he'd meet you there and lead the way to the Ballard pack lands, which is remote and inaccessible by vehicle."

I glanced over her to see Kent's eyes were still on the mobile phone in her hand as she read from the message.

"Call the rest of the team in," Thatch ordered, "and reach out to Jamison for an update. We need to make sure Blackheath isn't making an extra play."

"Got it," she said, casting me a brief look and nod. "I'll also reach out to the agent we had on Lucinda's detail."

With no sarcasm, no low hits, it was clear shit had just got real.

"Suit up, Callen. The two of us will head out to meet Laketon."

"Are the team coming with?" I asked.

Thatch shook his head. "No, just the two of us on the chopper. I want Jenson and Michaels all over Lentwood." He peered over at Kent as he made his way to the storage room Lucas had previously shown us. "Did you get a hit on the call, the location?"

Kent sounded pissed when she answered. "No, but we got a general location. Enough to keep the guys busy."

I followed after Thatch.

"Lucas." Thatch paused before I was sure he planned to help himself to Lucas's stash. "Are we good to go shopping?"

Lucas gave a small nod to the room of weapons. "You break it; you pay for it." He threw me a wink, and I forced myself to regulate my breathing. We all had this.

"Bill me," Thatch called over his shoulder as we entered the room, making Lucas chuckle, and I appreciated the attempted break from the fear raging through me.

It didn't take long before we were on a helipad four blocks away, courtesy of Kent being a certifiable magician. Headsets on, we sat, thighs deliberately touching. I needed the contact. I would have been surprised by how damn dependent I'd been of late, but this whole case was a shitshow that completely screwed with me. It was taking too long. And despite the connection between Thatch and me, and the perfect distraction he offered— not that he wasn't more than that—the loss of my sister, the need for revenge, and the concern for my niece were never far away.

I could bullshit with the rest of them, holding all three bubbling emotions hostage while I navigated the case and the relationship Thatch and I had eased into almost effortlessly.

Thatch's strong hand landed on my knee. I glanced

at it, brows lifting when I realised I'd been bouncing it up and down. "I feel like we're getting close," I said through the mic as I peered over at him.

He nodded. "I know this development is not one that we wanted as it involves Lucinda, but I agree, everything's coming together. We'll get it settled and shut this down once and for all."

The certainty behind his words eased through me, comforting me more than the heat from his hand.

"I need you to focus on Lucinda when we're there," Thatch instructed. I opened my mouth, planning to argue that I needed to find the bastards who were coming for her, but I didn't get the chance as Thatch continued speaking. "You need to make sure she's safe. Your focus will be shit unless you've got her."

Ignoring the likelihood he was right, I bristled, eyes narrowing. "I won't lose my focus."

For a moment, I thought he would roll his eyes at me, but I knew better. Instead, his jaw set into hard angles, and he leaned forward, despite me listening through the headset. "Let me make one thing clear. If you can't follow my orders on this, you can stay on the chopper."

The need to argue was on the tip of my tongue, but with the edge to his voice and the steel in his eyes, I knew he wasn't messing around. Not to get me wrong, he would have a damn fight on his hands if he tried to ground me, but it was time I couldn't waste wrestling for dominance.

I looked away first, not quite caring what he read that response to be. Thatch could be crazy intense and so fucking demanding. It was what made him so good at his job. The war between wanting to kiss him and make promises to him while telling him he could screw himself was savage. My heart, my gut, my mind were a mess. It was that reality right there that pulled me short. Control was essential for me to get this job done. It meant I had to suck up my pride and roll with it.

A deep exhale was the precursor for me finally saying, "I trust you."

The tension evaporated, and I glanced at Thatch to see his shoulder relaxed, yet his gaze remained on me. His eyes had softened. The firm grip he had on my thigh remained, and he squeezed. He didn't speak. He didn't have to.

Me though? Yeah, I had trouble keeping my mouth shut. "One day soon we'll be wrestling it out, you know." I didn't smile. There was jest in my words, but I spoke the truth and needed him to know it.

After the barest of glances at the pilot, Thatch's mouth descended on mine. It was clumsy and rushed. The heat and pressure made it hard to restrain myself and remember where we were. Fortunately, Thatch did that for us as he pulled back. He tugged the headset from my right ear, and his lips touched the shell of my ear when he said, "You tell me when and I'm there." The softest of kisses on my lobe followed. "I'm in this as much as you are." He then pulled back, and I had no idea how he had the restraint.

My cock hard, my need heady, I couldn't wait for the nightmare of the past few months to be over.

"We're almost there." Thatch nodded towards the window, and I saw a forest in the distance. It was vast and dense, and I had a moment of envy to wonder what life would be like out of the city with this as my playground.

I took the time to check my bag. I'd be carrying it when I shifted, so double-checked the weight distribution and everything was in order. Thatch started doing the same as the pilot signalled the two-minute ETA. Zipping my bag, I glanced at the flat greenery we were approaching. A vehicle was parked off to the side; Laketon, I assumed, since Thatch had touched base with him earlier in the flight.

As we descended, a large figure emerged from the SUV. The guy was greying and looked fit and strong if the bulk beneath his plaid shirt was anything to go by.

"Sure he's not a bear?"

Thatch shook his head, but I saw the twitch of his lips. "Just behave and try not to piss him off."

"Me?" I acted offended, knowing riling people up was something of a superpower of mine.

Thatch didn't bother responding as he hauled his bag, thanked the pilot, and jumped out of the chopper, head ducked as he strode towards Laketon. I followed suit and reached out to shake the man's hand after he finished greeting Thatch.

"You made good time," Laketon said, glancing at the two of us and probably trying to figure us out. Our short nods were answer enough as he continued. "You can throw whatever you're not taking in my car. We'll be heading north from here, about seven kilometres."

We started undressing and piling our stuff in Laketon's car.

"I already have three of my pack gone ahead. They're keeping a low profile as you wanted, making sure not to announce trouble. Debbie has Lucinda and says nothing is out of the norm."

I puffed out a breath, tension easing a little from the tightness in my shoulders. "Thanks. That's good," I said as Thatch reached out to take my jeans, brushing my fingers when he did so—his silent reminder we were in this together.

Butt naked and ready, we shifted quickly. My view

altered, closer to the land, and I had just enough time to appreciate Thatch in the final change. Pride for the man eased through me. Despite barely being a shifter for a couple of months, he changed like he was born to do it.

Giving in to temptation, I rubbed my head against his inky black fur while turning my attention to Laketon. His assessing eyes remained on us, no doubt taking in our change and reaction to each other. No judgment appeared in his eyes, just mild curiosity before he nodded, and we collected our bags in our mouths and raced north through the forest of gum trees.

CHAPTER 10

The unfamiliar scent of the Ballard pack filled my senses. While the forest's distinctive smell was easier to identify, it didn't overshadow the pack's unique hint of earth and minerals, though I couldn't identify which ones.

With the scent growing strong, I went on high alert. Not only did nervous energy of the possibility of attack ride me hard, but the anticipation of seeing my niece, scenting her for the first time, holding her tight as I broke her heart with the news about her mum kept me on edge.

She was the only true family I had left. There was Thatch who, with certainty, I could say I'd be making mine as soon as possible, but Lucinda would have the piece of my heart reserved for blood. And with that, I would do everything within my power to protect her.

On the outskirts, two men stood front and centre while three wolves flanked them. One woman and two other wolves remained off to the right. The three of us slowed, and immediately, it was clear that the woman and two wolves next to her were Laketon's. It meant one of the men was the alpha of this pack that was protecting my niece.

We stopped a respectable distance away before calling forward the change. I shifted first with Laketon a few seconds behind, and Thatch just a few behind him. Butt naked and rigid, I waited, hating the formality necessary. While I kept my eyes on the indigenous man whose alpha vibes rippled our way, I tuned into my other senses, trying like hell to make sure nothing and no one was coming up behind us.

The alpha nodded in greeting, saying, "Please dress. No need to stand on ceremony."

I bobbed my head in appreciation, and the three of us dressed quickly. Finally clothed, I refocused on the alpha.

"Laketon." The alpha's voice was strongly accented, much more so than the North Queensland of my youth and the less distinctive twang of Sydney dwellers. "Good to see you, my friend." Open and friendly, his tone had me relaxing. He stepped forward, Laketon mimicking his movements. They embraced, giving a friendly pat on each other's backs.

"Barwon, you too." Laketon stepped back.

Barwon's eyes then landed on me. "Callen." His hand clasped mine.

"Barwon," I greeted. "I can't thank you enough for caring for Lucinda." I allowed the depth of my words to flow through them. His protection meant everything.

"She's a good kid." His grip was firm, respectful, taking me by surprise. But my reality of packs and alphas was so different to the norm. There was no forced dominance in his handshake, no thread of power in his voice. I liked the man instantly.

I smiled for the first time since the rush of fear that had led me here. "She is." My heart lurched a little at the truth of my words and the gratitude I felt towards my sister for making sure that I was a familiar face and voice in my niece's life despite our distance. I stepped back and introduced Thatch, who'd held back and allowed me to take the lead.

"Why don't I take you to see Lucinda, and while you're catching up, Thatch, Laketon, and I can talk," he offered.

"That would be great, thanks."

He led us into what looked to be a community area,

at which point, the woman headed over and greeted Laketon with a hug. Seeing her up close, I was able to see their similarities in colouring and features, figuring she was his daughter.

"Annie told us what she knew when she arrived," Barwon said, pausing outside a large building. "And your agent, Daniels, continues to have eyes on Lucinda." Relief was a heady thing, but we were far from danger. His next words reminded me of that. "My pack has been alerted to the imminent threat and are on patrol. Don't let us being hidden away fool you into believing we're vulnerable or backwards." He grinned and reached out and took a tablet from the man by his side. "We have cameras and heat sensors spread out in a one-kilometre radius from our small town."

My brows rose in surprise. I glanced around and saw a large tower peeking through the tree canopy, recognising it for a communication tower.

After following my line of sight, Barwon clapped me on the back. "Much safer than the city, am I right?" His laugh was deep and friendly, and my resulting smile was easy.

"It's impressive," I agreed.

"These were the lands of my ancestors. They've always provided for us. The spirits are kind and protect us."

I nodded my understanding and made to speak but was caught off guard by the sound of pounding feet and a scent that immediately spoke to my heart. I zeroed in on the open doorway and immediately knelt at the appearance of a brown-haired girl with the same light brown eyes as her mother.

She launched herself at me. Her fierce hug immediately settled the dread that had ridden me hard since my sister's death.

"You're here," she said next to my ear, her hold on me not slackening. "Mummy said you'd come for me." My heart lurched at that, and I pressed a kiss to the top of her head before angling away just slightly.

"She said that?" I stared in wonder at the girl before me. She was so damn beautiful.

Wide-eyed, she nodded, her face becoming solemn. "She's not been here."

I bobbed my head, acknowledging her but remained silent, waiting to hear what she had to say.

"She said if ever she was gone for a long time that I shouldn't worry, as you would come for me."

I swallowed hard and didn't know if I could handle looking at the precious child in my arms. How could I destroy her world? Unable to speak just yet, I stood, still holding her close. Her head shifted to the side, and her eyes widened. I followed her gaze. Lucinda fixed her eyes on Thatch. He was a big guy without a doubt and could be intimidating as hell, especially to an eight-year-old, I was sure. On his face was an expression I hadn't seen before. Adoration bled from his soft, speckled green eyes as he smiled at my niece.

"Who are you?" Lucinda asked. Her voice was strong and held a confidence that made me smile.

Thatch edged forward within touching distance. "I'm Thatch."

Tilting her head as she gazed at him, the space between her brows formed the smallest of lines. "You smell a bit like Uncle Callen."

Both Thatch and I grinned at that, and a rightness settled in my chest that even though he wasn't fully mine, nor I his yet, we were cemented in each other's lives enough that our scents had mingled. Plus—

"And you smell a little like my mummy."

—there was that.

Pain arrowed through me, piercing my barely controlled restraint. I looked away from both of them, my eyes briefly meeting Laketon's. Seeing the pity, I shifted my gaze immediately. There was no doubt everyone here would understand my pain, but like hell would I break. Lucinda had to be at the centre of every decision and every emotion. I couldn't screw that up by being weak. That was unnegotiable.

I found my voice. "He smells good, right?" I smiled first at Lucinda, then at Thatch. "Why don't you show me around the place, and you can spend time with Thatch a little later?" Our conversation should be in private, and Thatch needed to take control of the situation with Lentwood.

"Okay." Her nod was followed up with both hands on my cheeks. "You have Mummy's eyes."

I grinned. "So do you." Setting her down, I looked at Barwon. "Am I good to let her show me around?" Courtesy dictated that I couldn't ignore the alpha's rule.

"Of course. Koen will stay close." He indicated a young shifter who was probably in his early twenties. "He's been helping taking care of young Lucinda." He winked at my niece. There'd also be Agent Daniels close by.

With a smile, she took my hand and said, "He's the best at hide and seek."

"Is that right?" I asked. "That's perhaps because you haven't played with me before." I ruffled her hair and then sent a smile of appreciation to Koen.

Amusement lit up his features, though, from his stance alone, I could see he remained vigilant. Any protector of Lucinda was someone who had my immediate respect.

"Come on then. Show me the way," I instructed. She

tugged at my hand and I sent a final look in Thatch's direction. Warmth filtered through me at the affection directed my way. There was no one else I would trust to take control of this than him. Since I needed my focus to be on my niece, he was the only man for the job.

TEARS NO LONGER STREAMED DOWN HER FACE, but small sobs had her body shuddering every couple of minutes. The evidence of her sadness saturated my T-shirt, and with no idea of how to comfort her any more, I simply held her close, dotting a kiss on her head after every quivering breath.

The crunch of dirt under a heavy boot had me looking up and past Koen, who had remained vigilant a few metres away. After making himself known to me, Agent Daniels had blended into the background, giving us some semblance of privacy. Despite the approaching steps, both men remained in position. I assumed they recognised the steps. My gaze landed on Barwon, by himself as he headed towards me.

Reaching my side, he offered a sad smile before placing a gentle hand on Lucinda's head. His eyes remained on mine when he said, "We have news. She will be safe with Koen. And that agent of yours is close by."

I nodded my understanding. "Thank you." Koen's soft footfalls headed our way as I stood with my niece still in my arms. "Are you okay to go with Koen?" I asked. She nodded and sniffed. With one more squeeze, I passed her over. Koen seemed to hold her effortlessly, and she went easily into his arms. A pang of envy hit me; I should have been here, forming that bond with her. I pulled myself up short, needing to get my head out of my arse. There was no time for regrets, and nothing I said or did could change where we were at. I fixed my gaze on the younger indigenous wolf. "Thank you. Take good care of her, please."

His smile was wide and friendly. "No worries. Lucinda here is my little *tidda*. Right, baby sister?" He stroked her head and she nodded against his chest. "I'll keep taking good care of her. She's like family." With that, he turned tail and headed back to the main area of the small settlement.

Alone with Barwon, I forced myself to bury my sadness and refocus. "What do you have?"

He eyed me a moment before speaking, his gaze penetrating and searching. After a beat, he asked, "When you leave, you'll be taking your niece?"

"Yes." While I hadn't discussed it with Thatch, there was no way I could leave without her. There was still my job and the current mission, but as soon as Lucinda had gripped me and trusted me enough with her grief, the certainty that we couldn't be apart again had taken me unaware but settled deep.

Barwon nodded. "Please take Koen with you."

Surprise had my eyes opening wide. "Koen?" My brows dipped low when I considered his request. "Why?" While it was obvious he thought of my niece as a little sister of sorts, for him to leave his pack to—I could only assume—help protect her was one hell of a move. And since I spoke from experience of the hardship of leaving a pack behind, even one I detested, I understood all too well what a big deal it was.

With modern times, there were lots of shifters like me who no longer belonged to a pack, usually those who opted to live in the city and choose a career in the SICB or similar. Living without a pack as a wolf shifter was hard. We took comfort in touch and bonding with our kin, and from the way they had welcomed and cared for Lucinda, the Ballard pack didn't appear to be rife with tension or bad blood.

"Koen is my nephew. His mother died during childbirth with him and his father died last year. He's a protector, could be an alpha, but he's also a loner. He would do well continuing his role of protector for your niece and living in your world. Moving away from the pressure of conforming to pack life is what he needs. His heart is no longer here."

Young Koen's plight was one I could appreciate. The only difference being, I *wished* my parents were dead. I exhaled and wasn't quite sure if I was doing the right thing, but I agreed. Having Koen help protect Lucinda was hardly a bad thing. Who the hell knew what he'd do with himself, or even where he'd stay, but screw it. Nothing about the past few weeks made a lick of sense. We'd figure it all out eventually.

"Thank you." Barwon reached out and shook my hand. "Your Thatcher is waiting for us." I raised my brows at that and reacted to his smirk with a smile. "Let's walk."

We headed towards a cabin complete with wraparound veranda. "Has he received any more intel from base?" I asked, unable to keep quiet and wait till I was with Thatch.

"Yes, but we've also received a call from my friend about twenty kilometres away. Two unfamiliar vehicles were heading in our direction."

I nodded, recognising that for such an isolated place, anything outside the norm would be reported.

"Eight men in total, but we're not sure of species."

"And they'll have to come by foot the same sort of distance we did?" I clarified.

"Yes. I have a couple heading out to keep an eye on their location. We've also relocated a portion of our pack to keep them out of danger, but we don't plan for these men to get as close as our settlement."

I could understand why he wouldn't want that. "Has Thatch explained what these men are after, what they're doing?"

Anger sparked in his eyes as he looked at me. "Yes. And we'll do what we can here to stop this from happening."

Gratitude for Barwon and his pack had me pausing. He stopped and faced me. "Thank you. I'm not sure how I'll be able to repay you."

"Help my nephew find the life and happiness he is searching for, and balance will be restored. Some journeys take kin away, never to return. Our ancestors walked so much of our land; I'm sure over to Sydney too." He smiled. "He'll find his peace there. You'll help him."

I kept my face neutral, wondering what the hell I'd gotten myself into, but it was too late to react now. Instead, I bobbed my head and continued.

We met inside the cabin, my gaze settling immediately on Thatch, whose eyes were on me as I stepped through the door. He didn't miss a beat as he said to Laketon, "We need to leave in five minutes. No later."

My pulse spiked. This had to be done right. It didn't matter that this was going down now and our team didn't surround us. The case may have been personal to Thatch and me, but it was personal to every shifter too. It meant that I had to have faith in Laketon and Barwon.

Barwon stepped further into the room and began dishing out orders to his shifters while Thatch reached my side and indicated I should follow him out. Alone and heading a short distance away from the building, I inhaled and exhaled slowly, allowing myself a moment to pull myself together before I needed to refocus completely.

"You're great with her."

I swept my hand over my face and back through my hair. "You can't know that."

Thatch's brow quirked high. "Her greeting of you, an uncle she's never met in real life, was enough of a clue. And that she's been at the centre of every decision you've made is more than enough."

I watched his face carefully when I said, "After we take care of these bastards, she's coming back to Sydney with me."

One step closer and a firm hand on my cheek with the words "With us," had my heart pounding loudly. The sound made it difficult to hear anything. It beat too loud, too ferocious in reaction to his declaration. The talk that had never happened nudged itself into my brain, but it seemed talking about feelings and shit was unnecessary. Thank Christ. We were both men of action, and I'd never been more grateful for the fact.

I allowed myself a small smile and leaned into his strong palm. "Sounds good."

A nod was all he gave as he stepped back. "Three minutes and we're out of here."

A new wave of tension flooded me as we rushed towards our bags that were filled with the weapons we'd packed. I stripped quickly beside Thatch.

"We plan to ambush southeast of here." Just then, we heard the crackle of static from a two-way and listened in. One of Barwon's men explained that there were at least two vamps and two lions. But they were yet to get a read on the others. When he said that they were slow going and unfamiliar with the route, I grinned.

Barwon and Laketon stepped out with a group of shifters, eight men and two women. Laketon's smile was almost sardonic. I couldn't help but grin back.

"Their slow progress means we can get behind them if we move fast." Laketon pulled off his shirt as he spoke.

My gaze landed on Barwon. I had no idea how old the alpha was, but grey streaked his dark hair. His eyes connected with mine. "Don't even think about it. There's more than enough life left in me yet." Humour lit his voice, but strength carried his words, making them ring true.

"I didn't say anything," I said, hands held palm out towards him.

"One minute," Thatch said.

A ripple in the air indicated the changes taking place. With my wolf vision, it was easy to appreciate the strength of the shifters. None would have the disciplined training of Thatch or me, but that didn't mean shit. Not when they lived remotely and read the land so much better than I ever could.

Clamping down on the bag's straps, I flicked my head as the weight landed on my back, my teeth keeping a firm grip. A wolf who, as a man, was tall, dark, and built with sinewy muscle took point. I'd scented him as Barwon's beta, but had no clue of his name.

Together, we raced through the forest, following paths well-travelled before darting off route unexpectedly. Over downed trees and across creeks we kept a solid speed. Any other time I would have appreciated the freedom I could taste in the air being so far away from the city, but my ears constantly listened for noises that didn't fit. My gaze, while travelling between the beta and Thatch's three wolves in front of me, remained vigilant of changing shadows and erratic movements in my periphery.

My ears registered the change of pace before my eyes. We slowed and switched direction, noticeably keeping to the same paw falls. After a couple more minutes, the beta paused, and we followed suit. He shifted, and Thatch followed. Anticipation pulsated through me as I waited for direction from Thatch.

"We're expecting the vampires to be on the drug I explained earlier. Keep vigilant and don't take one on by yourself," he whispered. Protocol indicated we'd stop a minimum of one and a half kilometres from hostiles for low conversations and checks when shifters and vamps were present, and specifically in the open. A change in wind direction could quite possibly carry a voice a little too far and screw it all up.

"Laketon, John"—who I figured was the beta—"Tallis, Neil, Tom, and Kasey will shift into human form and stick with me. The rest will stay shifted. Leave your gear twenty metres from interception in case you need to shift. We'll target the vampires."

A growl rippled through the air, a warning that I didn't like this plan. The last time Thatch went up against a vampire resulted in an injury and me being scared shitless. Thatch's eyes slammed into mine, hard, unrelenting. He wasn't moving on this. Bastard. But for all we knew, there could be more than two vampires. What then?

Thatch's hard stare moved past me, churning my gut while pissing me off. If he got himself hurt, I'd lay him out. A humourless snort filled the air. This time Thatch's gaze returned to me, and he rolled his eyes. Yeah, I was sure the arsehole could read my mind.

"Focus on the shifters and any humans," he continued, speaking to the rest of us. "I know our intel isn't perfect, but there's no way we're letting them move closer to the Ballard pack." Nods and soft snorts of agreement followed from the shifters a moment before the changes took place. The team dressed, armed themselves with rifles rather than the handguns and technologically advanced weapons SICB used, and waited.

"Kent's organised a pickup at our previous drop-off point for any hostiles we take." Growls of dissent followed. I got it. Seriously. Sometimes following the rules of the SICB sucked arse. "But do not put yourself at unnecessary risk to simply immobilize."

My brows sprang high at that. While I hadn't known Thatch when he was human, I could imagine he played by the rules... mainly. There were some titbits of gossip I'd wrangled out of Jenson, but nothing was at the level of taking lives.

Me, however, there was a reason why I was a pain in Brent's arse beyond him apparently having an issue with shifters and the confusing BS connection between him and my father. Mainly because of the extra paperwork I caused.

Before Thatch gave the go, he sent me the briefest of glances. I tried like hell to get him to mind-read, to send him a message telepathically that when we got out of this, which we seriously were, I was going to screw him so damn hard he'd be walking bow-legged for days. There may have been some warm and fuzzy feelings at play too. But it was best to focus on the immediately gratifying element of this connection we had.

It didn't take long to reach the point of picking up the sound of the group trampling through the forest. For shifters and vamps, they were noisy bastards. A few more metres, and I placed my bag on the ground. Anticipation swept through me, sending a vibration of determination in its wake.

They were going down.

Laser-focussed, I zeroed in on my first target—the largest shifter of the bunch. A lion. At some point, the SICB would need to investigate why there were so many lions involved in the creation of the drugs. It had to be more than basic greed, right?

A glance at Barwon, and I indicated who I was taking down. He swung his gaze to the shifter to the lion's right, then seemed to have a similar conversation with his wolves. The exchange was brief, barely seven seconds, and just in time. I raced towards my target. It was as my jaw clamped around the back of his neck, that the vamp I was sure Thatch would be targeting lifted his head.

Fierce growls erupted, along with snarls and tears of flesh. I was aware of a whimper but kept my focus on the blood filling my mouth. They fought back. The bites brutal, speed staggeringly fast, and with a savagery that sent me on high alert. A shot was fired, and I knew there were going to be no survivors. This crew of mercenaries would not be laying down their weapons and going quietly.

A swift twist, and the lion slumped to the ground. I allowed myself the briefest of moments to take in the scene and see where I was needed. One of Barwon's wolves was bloody and limping, but still assisting another in taking down an enemy wolf. There was a human prone on the leafy ground, and a vampire dead.

With four more to go, I attempted to identify who was the greatest threat, but froze when I only saw three fighting forms. Eyes on Laketon, who had taken a hit that left him a safe few metres from his battle with a vamp, Tallis and Kasey still hitting hard, I shifted, calling out, "Where's the fourth?" A cement weight dropped in my gut, and I growled, "Where's Thatch?"

Laketon wiped blood from his mouth and spared me

the barest of glances, saying, "He and Tom went after another vamp. Bastard was wiry."

Barely contained fear merged with anger-threaded heat as I demanded, "Where?"

"Headed west, towards the Ballard pack."

"Fuck."

I turned my back as Laketon reentered the fray and called to Barwon, "You hear that?"

The deep brown eyes of his wolf form stared at me intently. He yipped, and John's voice filtered over the grunts and feral snarls. "We're good. You go."

Laketon dipped his head and took off as I willed myself to shift faster than I ever had before. Not stopping for my bag, not willing to slow myself down, I raced after Barwon and soon took the lead. Racing in the general direction of the pack land took me to a downed tree where I finally picked up Thatch's unique scent.

I pushed harder. Faster. My paws carried me through the brush, the pounding of my steps and the cracking of twigs and rustle of leaves letting anyone or anything who listened know that I was on a mission. And I didn't care who heard. This wasn't a time for stealth.

A grunt up ahead, perhaps five hundred metres or so, alerted me of Thatch's position. I charged forward, only slowing down when I heard the distinctive crunch of bone and a piercing howl. A slower approach was necessary so I wouldn't make things even worse. But the desire to dash in and save the day rode me hard.

Once my eyes adjusted to the scene before me, heaviness settled in my chest. Charging in would put Thatch and Tom at risk. They had the vamp penned in. And unless the vampire had mastered the ability of teleportation, he was screwed.

Wide, feral eyes focused on Thatch. There was no doubt the vamp was drugged up to the eyeballs. Vesper, I assumed. The predator in him was at the surface, making the vicious killer in him even deadlier. I saw Thatch move at the same moment the vamp did.

Screw this.

Tense muscles drove me forward. The need to intercept the hit on Thatch pushed me beyond any desire for self-preservation. There was no way I'd get my jaw around the vamp's neck though, so I went for his side. Sharp teeth found purchase in the vampire's flesh, preventing the vampire's hand from gripping Thatch's throat.

A duck and a roll had Thatch bouncing back to his feet while I held on for dear life. Ignoring the pain from the strong grip on my skull proved difficult as hell. The bastard was going to crush my skull unless I made a break for it or took him down. Before I loosened my jaw, Thatch struck hard; at the same time, Tom clutched at the vampire's neck, and Barwon clamped his sharp teeth on the vampire's arm that held my skull in his grip.

Pain shot through me and a yelp ripped free, but I couldn't break away. I shook my head, and with the help of Barwon's determined grip, broke free. No longer feeling like my brain was going to explode, I tore into the vampire's side.

Spots danced in my vision as I forced my jaw closed, then tugged, hard. Flesh came away, not helping my already spinning brain. I spat flesh and blood out fast. Hell knew what would happen if I ingested the stuff.

Ignoring my blurring vision, I went back for more. Purpose propelled me forward just as the three shifters dragged the vampire to his knees. Bones crunched. Blood filled my mouth. The final scream left the vampire's mouth as I tore away his throat.

It was done.

And not a moment too soon, as I was going to black out. I took a final glance at Thatch, knowing he was going to be pissed as hell. The sound of his voice as he called my name drifted through me, not quite finding purchase as blackness took me.

I HAD NO IDEA HOW MUCH TIME HAD PASSED, but there was a soft mattress under my back, and other than a headache that rivalled any hangover I'd ever had, I was confident I was whole. And safe. Thatch's scent filled my nose, and if it wasn't for the pain behind my eyes, I would have opened them to look my fill. A glimpse at Thatch right now would be the best kind of medicine.

"I need you to drink." Steel painted Thatch's words. Perhaps my prediction of him being pissed wasn't accurate. Nope. Pissed wasn't even close. He sounded furious to the point of enraged. I huffed air through my nostrils and figured there was a bowl of water before me. But that meant lifting my head.

Soft hands at my head helped me up. At the touch, I felt the tremor in them. "Okay," he said, softer this time. "You should be good."

Eyes firmly shut, I lolled out my tongue and lapped. The movement didn't help the pain, but the cold water filling my mouth, my throat, my gut was refreshing. I paused a moment and would have angled my head in question if I were able.

"Pain medication," Thatch answered, no doubt reading my stillness.

After I took my fill, I heard the bowl moved, and I sighed contently when he placed my head gently down, following with a soft stroke. He couldn't be that angry with me if he was petting me, right?

"Do you think you can shift?"

While I knew I could, I wasn't sure if I was up for what followed. Thatch ripping me a new one, the likely pressure in my head? Neither sounded desirable. It was the sound of Lucinda's voice coming from a distant room that had me sucking up the change. She had to know I was okay.

The change took longer than usual as I eased through the transition so that I didn't vomit and humiliate myself in the process. Panting and sweating, I lay flat on the mattress, eyes still closed.

A click of a switch followed by "Light's off" was the last nudge for me to open my eyes. After the initial ache that became a dull throb, my focus veered to Thatch. I would have grimaced from the look sent my way if I was feeling braver. Not being able to handle more discomfort, I stilled and forced my eyes to remain fixed to his.

The situation reversed, I would have already lain into him, my fear driving my fury. His silence was deafening.

Breaking, I rubbed my chest and said, "It wasn't like I could stand back." There was no heat in my words. Honestly, they sounded weak to me.

The silence thickened, meaning that my discomfort grew by the second. I hated the quiet, detested holding back. With that driving me, I added, "You would have done the same." While there was no real challenge in my tone, there wasn't a chance he could deny it. Perhaps he would have thought things out a bit better, as, let's be real, I was something of a hothead, but still, the outcome would have been the same.

He didn't fidget, didn't even clench his damn jaw; instead, he edged closer, stopping at the point where his warm breath brushed against my skin. So close, the green in his eyes was visible in the darkened room, the whites of his eyes a perfect contrast to his deep brown skin, all detectible despite the sun being kept at bay by the blacked-out curtains. When Thatch lowered his head, his forehead gently touching mine, my muscles uncoiled. Held-back tension worked its way out my limbs, easing my head, though driving my heart crazy, but for different reasons than my discomfort.

"You mustn't ever get dead," he whispered.

My breath caught at the vulnerability in his words. "Right back at ya," I murmured, angling my head back, tempting him to move and take what was his.

He groaned before our mouths even connected. I got it. I really did.

This unspoken sex ban or extended rain check or whatever the hell it was drove me to distraction. His tongue in my mouth, our lips caressing each other's, the hardening between my legs, only one way existed to fix this.

I latched onto his zipper and tugged sharply, shoving my hand in his pants, shifting his briefs out of the way and tugging his length out. He broke the kiss. Dilated eyes peered back at me, filled with heat and need. A hiss escaped his kiss-swollen mouth when I stroked. "This abstinence shit is ridiculous," I mumbled before stroking harder and faster. He bucked in my hand and pressed his face to my neck, kissing my skin and alternating between small bites and licks. "I can't take it anymore."

His moan edged towards savage as he sidled closer to me, his hand skirting down my chest and under the loose sheet. The tent I created left plenty of room for him to grasp me firmly. With the increased pounding of my heartbeat echoing in my ears, I almost missed it when he said, "If we're quick, I could ride you."

Wide-eyed, I pulled my head out of the lust riding me hard to stare at him. I needed him to be serious. Needed to make sure we could do this. "Quick or a marathon, I don't give a damn. I just need inside you."

Thatch pulled away abruptly, tearing off his clothes and exposing every mouth-watering inch of skin to me. I made to ask about lubrication—relieved we no longer needed to worry about protection, since he was no longer human—when the sound of Lucinda's voice stopped me cold. Frozen, I looked at Thatch in horror. I was sure my cock was going to fall off if I didn't get any soon.

Surprising me again, Thatch leaned in, his gaze roaming my body as he pulled the sheet away. Bobbing away, completely ignoring that my niece was close by, my dick didn't give a damn. "The door's locked, but you'll need to be quiet."

Hell yes.

My grin was wide as I snagged hold of his arm. "Lube," I managed to grunt, despite struggling to contain my desire.

Swooping his jeans off the floor, he tugged a bottle out of his pocket. I raised my brows high, not even caring the action sliced pain through my head. "Came prepared. That's a fucking fine quality in a man."

His sexy smirk made my heart beat faster as he angled over me, sitting on my thighs. My smile dropped as I placed my shaky hands on his bare skin. We'd danced around this moment, fear holding me back, which was probably the same as his reasons.

When his gaze dropped to my lips, they tingled in anticipation, desperate for more. "We haven't got much time."

His eyes dilated at that, just as he wrapped his firm hand around me. My eyes rolled back in my head. There was a good chance this would impact my healing and I'd hurt like hell later, but there wasn't a chance I couldn't let this happen.

A slick coat was spread on me, Thatch's hands sure and steady. Half-mast eyes peered down at me. "You want to do me?"

My lips quirked upwards. "Don't I ever."

His lips twitched as he squirted the lube on my waiting hand.

"Lift," I instructed. He did so, and just as I edged closer and finally made contact to prepare him as fully as possible with the time ticking by too damn fast, his lips pressed against mine in a fervent kiss. There was no more time for words. Not holding back, my tongue worked in tandem with my fingers. Intoxicated by his taste, his proximity, the knowledge that any moment now, I'd be buried balls deep, I sucked on his tongue before breaking the kiss and squeezing his hips. "You ready?" I whispered, unsure how I'd keep from howling.

"So ready." He took control as he held onto my wrists and positioned himself over me. Slowly easing down, his eyes remained on mine with a laser focus. I grunted as he exhaled and held back from thrusting up. Just as I thought I would explode from the need to be buried to the hilt, he bottomed out. Our groans came out in unison. I smiled, and he mirrored the action before he clasped my hands and rose off me.

Determined to keep my eyes on him, desperate to not miss a thing, I tried to absorb every sensation. The tightness, the rightness, the way a sweat bead formed on his brow and trickled down, all urged me to move. I could no longer remain still, needing to pick up the pace and drive him harder, bury myself in him so deep, there'd be no coming back from this for either of us.

If there was such a thing as a mate or fate, he'd be wrapped up so far in my fantasy, I'd be celebrating from the rooftops that he was mine. Instead, I had the way he clung to me, the way his heart picked up speed and settled at the same rate as mine.

That was enough.

Better than any damn fantasy.

Getting close, I slid one hand that gripped his hip to his pelvis. Heat and steel, a heady combination, felt perfect in my grip as I worked him.

Thatch grunted and whispered, "Harder."

Both my hand and my hips moved double time, my aim to take him over the edge before I exploded and saw stars. My toes curled and I had no choice but to close my eyes as my orgasm slammed into me. Somehow managing to keep jacking him off, relief swelled through when his warm release covered my hand.

Shuddering beneath him, I pulled him towards me. He was already on his way. His mouth connected with mine before I could take a full breath. He angled away, and I opened my eyes. "If that doesn't fix your head, nothing will." His mouth quirked up at the sides, his eyes still half-mast, my own almost foggy in the wake of my orgasm.

I snorted, and he winced. Firm hands clamped down on me. "Don't do that. Fuck, Callen, you're going to break your dick off."

Another snort followed. This time my shaking shoulders joined in as I laughed harder.

"Shit, fuck, stop."

"I can't help it." I winced, despite my laughter. My flagging dick was far too sensitive to handle him still gripping me so tightly. "You need help getting up?" Genuine concern filled my question, but by Thatch's scowl, it was clear my amusement covered it.

"Just stay still."

I nodded, biting my lip and trying not to move a muscle. But bloody hell, the concentration on his face, the scent of sex and sweat and our combined essence had me twitching inside him.

Thatch's brow shot high. "You're serious?"

I risked a shrug.

"You wait till it's my turn to top, wisearse."

"It's your arse—"

When his large hand covered my mouth, I stuck my

tongue out and licked his palm. With a shake of his head, Thatch leaned down and removed his palm, planting a quick kiss on my mouth. "You can't help yourself, can you?"

Contentment filtered through me, and I admitted, "Not when it comes to you, no."

His eyes softened at my words, making my heart do a weird flip. Thatch was hard, serious, and kept his own counsel most of the time, but it was these growing moments when he let me in that had the power to bring me to my knees. "Come on," he said quietly. "I can hear your niece almost pacing a hole in the floor a couple of rooms over. Any longer, and Koen's just going to let her loose."

That was enough incentive to get us both moving and back to the real world.

CHAPTER 11

All the mercenaries were dead. Neil had been injured but was close to recovery, and Kent had sent in the news that Brent was MIA. It left Thatch with a decision I knew went against the grain. He had bodies, yet couldn't call in and report the incident. We all knew it was too risky, especially as we remained unsure whether Brent was working alone in the agency.

We stayed until the afternoon due to a combination of the return of my headache after post-coital bliss that had made me vomit, and getting Lucinda ready to go, along with Koen. With an entourage from the Ballard Pack and Laketon, we were escorted to the waiting chopper, Agent Daniels in tow.

So much had happened in the last thirty hours or so, and I was bone tired. A gentle squeeze of my hand had me glancing down at my niece. She was so bloody brave. Her excitement at going on a helicopter, her happiness over finally meeting me, and her relief at having Koen by her side warred with her grief. Soon after she shared a smile or a hint of joy, sadness quickly followed, flittering through her light brown eyes.

Wide-eyed, Lucinda peered up at me. "We are closing the door, right?"

A furrow between my brows appeared when I asked, "What do you mean?"

A quick flick of her eyes to the helicopter before returning to me gave me an inkling, and when she said, "In the movies, the doors are always open, and I might fall out. My feet and paws like the ground," I struggled to hold back my laughter.

"I think it can be arranged to have doors closed."

Relief had her grinning and calling out to Koen, "It's okay. It won't be like that movie where people fell out. We'll be safe."

Koen pursed his lips before nodding his approval. "That's a relief, all right. You had me worried there." A mischievous wink followed before he looked at me, straightening a little, his smile slipping.

I couldn't quite figure the guy out. He was great with Lucinda, and while I'd dug a little deeper after my sexcapades with Thatch to discover more of Koen's story, I needed to work out myself who he really was and what the hell I should do with him.

I turned a final time to Laketon. "Thank you again," I said as I shook his hand once more.

"You'll let us know if you need anything and when you've put the mongrels down, yeah?"

I bobbed my head and withdrew my hand. "I will." My sister had made the right choice reaching out to her old friend, which had brought her to Laketon and his pack. While it hadn't saved her, it had saved her daughter. It was also a reminder that all packs weren't criminal pieces of crap.

"Let me take that." Thatch swooped up the bag next to my feet, and I quirked my brow.

"Really?"

He shrugged. "I can be chivalrous if I want."

I snorted. "I'll remind you of that the next time I need to clean the bathroom."

He rolled his eyes. "Since when have you cleaned the bathroom since living with me?" Amusement filled his voice. "I have a housekeeper."

"Who I've still never met. I think you have a weird secret fetish that involves you—"

"What, cleaning the house at some crazy hour and secretly being able to cook?"

A smirk lifted my lips. "There have to be more things

that you're not great at beyond cooking." For real, Thatch was the epitome of perfect. My eyes took on a will of their own as they lazily drifted over his mighty fine form. When I returned to his face, tension filled his features, but he couldn't mask the hunger in his eyes.

Hell yes. I kinda loved that he reacted so easily and quickly to me. A guy could get used to that.

"Okay, you lot," Laketon said, pulling our attention to him and the laughter in his voice. "It's time to be getting the hell out of here and getting everything dealt with."

Right, the mission. I nodded and led Lucinda to the waiting chopper. Within a few minutes, we were loaded and heading back to Sydney.

Without a doubt we were heading back to Lucas's rather than the SICB. At some point, we'd need to bring in Durrant, but we first had to figure out where the arsehole was.

As soon as we settled in Lucas's safehouse-slash-warehouse, he led Lucinda and Koen away to the living quarters of the space, hooking them up with a TV and showing them where they could get food. There was also a small outside area with a basketball hoop, which would keep them entertained. I gave Lucas a grateful nod of thanks when he came back. "They okay?"

"Yeah," he said as he retook his seat at the main console. "Movies and popcorn, and they're golden."

"Thank you."

"All good. I'll find a way for you to pay me back."

Without a doubt he would too.

"So, you and boss man are playing daddies now?" Kent said, completely changing the subject while sporting a wry grin. "That didn't take long to have your own ready-made family."

She knew the situation, knew the reality and the whys, so rather than getting pissy at her jibe, I responded how I always did to her. With a middle finger and a "And I've already contacted Jada, who said you'll be the first to volunteer for babysitting duties."

When she froze and a look of horror crossed her face, I grinned.

"You better be joking."

I tugged out my phone and threw together a quick text to Jada, whose number I'd managed to wrangle a couple of weeks ago just to piss Kent off. After I hit Send, I stared at the screen, seeing glorious dots appear and dance around a little. Jada's message popped up. "Not anymore." If I wasn't careful, Kent would kick my arse, but it was totally worth it, especially when she appeared nauseous when I added, "Jada said, and I quote 'of course, we'll look after Lucinda. Anytime you want. Just let Kent know. I know she'd love to help out.'"

"You rangy bastard." I had just enough time to duck the incoming wireless mouse she threw at my head. My laughter followed and abruptly stopped when Thatch stepped into the room, his face stricken.

On high alert, I asked, "What's happened?"

"It's Jenson." He didn't have to say anything else for us to understand; the pain contorted with anger was enough. But still he elaborated. "He's dead." No, *he's gone* or *lost*. No, *he's not with us anymore*. There was no room for misinterpretation.

Despite only knowing the human agent for a couple of months or so, distress lanced through me, tangling with fury. It would be only a fraction of how hard this development would hit both Thatch and Kent. And fuck, Michaels. "What about Michaels? What details do you have?"

"He's okay. Heading here now. He's just left the hospital." A quiet strength filled Thatch's words. He was made to lead, to have me bowing at his damn feet with how truly incredible he was. But the pain ebbed off him in waves, cutting me deep. I hated his pain, the loss, the whole cluster of destruction Lentwood, with Brent and my father, had created.

They all needed to be in the ground. And whoever had taken Jenson out needed to be first.

"Michaels said it was Brent. We even have it on camera," he elaborated.

Kent snarled "The piece of mother—" ended abruptly as she clamped her hand over her mouth, and I just knew it was to hold back a sob. She thrust her head back, face to the ceiling, and seemed to be exhaling a breath she didn't need. The combined hurt in the room made my hackles rise. Just like my sister had deserved the time to be properly mourned, this too would have to wait until we settled this.

"Are we going to Durrant with this?" I asked, not sure which way Thatch would go and having no idea how we could keep it from her.

His jaw tensed before he said, "No."

Every single person in the room bobbed their heads in agreement. Durrant involved would mean we'd have to take him in alive.

He continued. "Michaels has already spun a story to keep her out of the loop, but we won't have long before she comes to us for answers."

There was only so long you could keep an agent's death hidden, and doing so went against the grain. Jenson had a family, but we all knew he'd wanted this case over and the perps buried. So we'd spin the necessary tales to make sure that happened.

"Now's the time to walk." Thatch's voice was clear and firm and held no room for negation.

Lucas, Kent, and I headed to the large table, each pulling out a seat. We all turned as one towards Thatch. We were all in this. My heart kicked up, worry for Thatch peeking up. I'd broken so many rules since joining the SICB, I was constantly surprised I hadn't been fired. And while I loved my job, my role, it wouldn't break me if I left. But Thatch... this was all he'd known, and he excelled at it. As if hearing my inner worry, Thatch's gaze moved to mine and stayed.

One simple nod was sent my way. It was enough. He knew what he was risking, and was all in. Screw the consequences.

"Okay," he said as he pulled out a chair and sat. "Kent, can you pull up the footage from the coordinates Michaels should have sent over?"

"All over it." She leaned over and snagged the tablet from the table she'd been working at. Her fingers flew over the screen, and we all looked over at the large screen positioned central to the table and fixed to the wall. "Got it."

We watched with various levels of horror and outrage as Brent shot Jenson from behind while he was sweeping the building. Jenson had gone down hard, was out and dead, unable even to get a call in. Within seconds, Brent had grabbed a case off a unit and high-tailed it out of there. It took four minutes for Michaels to find Jenson, and I was sure I wasn't the only one to appreciate we couldn't hear the wail from Michaels.

The screen stilled when Kent pulled up another camera, this time showing Brent getting in a Prado, complete with the number plate showing.

Silence pulsed through the room, my and Thatch's shallow breaths making sporadic slices through the quiet. It was Lucas who spoke first. "This your man who's arrived?" A few buttons later, live footage of the main entrance replaced the still screen of the dead man walking.

Thatch cleared his throat before saying, "Yeah, that's Michaels."

Wordlessly, Lucas bobbed his head and pressed the necessary command to let Michaels in the building.

"Kent, make sure that footage is only accessible by us until further notice," Thatch instructed.

Four sets of eyes zeroed in on the door as Michaels entered. Grief rolled off him. The steel in his eyes was familiar. Bloody determination was one hell of a catalyst to get the job done. Silently, he joined the table and sat, his eyes moving around the four of us before settling on Lucas, the one face he didn't know.

"Mathew Lucas," Lucas said, and dipped his head in acknowledgement.

Michaels's body all but vibrated with tension as he nodded back before turning his attention to Thatch. He doggedly ignored Kent.

"Kent," I said, needing to move forward, "how are those plates looking?"

"Running them now," she said.

I nodded, ignored how her voice pitched strangely. "Thatch, you heard from Jamison?"

"Nothing," he answered. "I'll call now for an update." He stood and moved a few metres away from the table.

My gaze landed on Lucas. "Lucas, what's the latest on Lentwood?"

Frustration squeezed his brows tightly together as he admitted, "Nothing. The guy's a damn ghost."

I let the irony of that statement, considering the anonymity of Thatch's unit, brush past me. "We need to get eyes on Brent. He wasn't in his vehicle." I directed my question to Lucas. "Did he find the bugs?"

He was already shaking his head before I finished talking. "No chance. They were undetectable." He glanced at his tablet, saying, "Hold on."

I risked a glance at Michaels. His eyes were on the blank screen on the wall. There was no doubt he was listening, but it was clear he needed to get himself together.

"Okay," Lucas said, a sardonic smile appearing on his lips, "his car's parked near the docks." A moment later, footage appeared on the screen.

"What other angles do you have?" I asked.

Fast fingers moved over the screen before multiple angles appeared in their own split boxes. There had to be something here. This was well out his way. What had taken him there? Alertness drummed through me. "How far away were you from the docks, Michaels?"

His head whipped in my direction. "Maybe twelve kilometres."

"And why there?" I pushed.

"He'd taken an earlier call and agreed to pick up something from there." Michaels's eyes fixed firmly on mine. "Jenson was closer to the collection point and got there before me. The fucker didn't wait." A clenched fist smashed against the table. "Always so fucking gung-ho." He shook his head, his distress thick in the air.

My pain recognised his, but I had to shut that shit down fast. "Do we know what the collection was?"

"Vesper," he answered.

Confusion swept through me. "He's collecting the

drugs?" I shook my head. "This doesn't make sense. We thought his involvement was due to his contacts, right? Hooking Lentwood up, and what, passing on intel of our and others' investigations?"

Lucas spoke up. "The call came through about midday. We suspect Lentwood by now knows that you have your niece and the fodder he sent are all out of the picture."

"They're relocating." A large container ship caught my attention. "Can you zoom in on screen six?"

The live footage of the container and its surrounds filled the screen. There was plenty of activity—loader and forklifts zipping in and out as a large crane positioned huge containers onboard. "What's that on the right-hand side of the ship?"

Lucas pressed a few keys to show us as Thatch returned to the table, his phone in his hand and his muscles taut.

"Helicopter pad," I said, then focussed on Thatch, who clearly had something to report.

"Jamison's said that Blackheath never returned. They've since got a lead that he's on a flight to Sydney. He and his team are heading here now."

I fisted my hands. "What time is the ETA?"

Lucas spoke up as he typed something on his screen. "Their plane has just departed, while Blackheath should be arriving in Sydney within ten minutes or so. It's a privately chartered flight."

Looking over at Thatch, I worked hard to bite my tongue and let him take point. It surprisingly wasn't as difficult as I expected it to be. Though, my throbbing head that still hadn't quite settled perhaps had something to do with that.

"Lucas," Thatch said, "I'm going to need you on the ground with us. That okay?"

He was nodding before Thatch had finished talking. "Sure thing."

Turning his attention to Kent, Thatch instructed, "Are you good to direct us from here?"

"Abso-freakin'-lutely," Kent answered. "Lucas has shown me where all of the good tech is." She grinned salaciously.

I scrunched my nose. "Your hard-on over tech is mildly disturbing."

She barely cut her eyes to me, already elbow-deep in whatever she was doing. Though a quick flip of her middle finger made me grin.

"Michaels." Thatch's voice remained balanced, clear, and devoid of inflection. Colour me impressed. I had no idea how he managed it. Just looking at Michaels made me both pissed off and sad. "You're with me while Lucas is with Callen. Stick close," he ordered.

His pairings made sense. Lucas and I had worked together for years. While he'd spent a lot of time in my ear, we'd shared hours' worth of mission time together on the ground too.

"We'll get Jamison to meet us at the docks."

I waited for the pang of jealousy and smiled smugly when it didn't hit. My somewhat crazed, self-impressed smile had Thatch pausing briefly, I imagined wondering what the hell was wrong with me. I shrugged, indicating he should continue. It was amazing what good old sex could achieve—the destruction of jealousy apparently high on the list with a happy penis.

"We won't be moving until we have eyes on Lentwood. He's our priority." Thatch glanced around our team.

"What about Brent?" Michaels croaked.

I added, "And Blackheath?"

"They're targets too, but we need to cut this operation off at the head. The rest will soon fall. If we can take them on at the same time, we go for it and can celebrate with a Bundy rum or five by tomorrow. If not, we'll catch up with them." Confidence anchored Thatch's words.

"And reading Durrant in?" Kent asked. "This will all need to be handled tonight, with Brent's involvement," she challenged.

"She's right," I added. "I understand why you're saying Lentwood needs to be the main target, but if you don't want Durrant involved, it's got to happen today. Tonight." I tapped my fingers on the table. "Lucas, have you heard any chatter about Brent?" To be honest, we were all surprised as hell Durrant didn't already know and hadn't charged in to take over the investigation. Or at least get involved, since she would have likely tasked Thatch's team with the mission.

"Brent covered his tracks and applied for leave." Head bent over his tablet, Lucas read a moment before saying, "He put emergency cover in six hours ago, on the grounds of his sister falling ill."

"Does he even have a sister?" Kent asked before I could voice the same question.

"Give me a second." Lucas's fingers flew across the keyboard. As he did so, I cast a glance at Thatch. He looked weary despite the tension keeping his muscles taut. In his focussed state, he looked every bit the leader, and I was man enough to admit how incredibly sexy he was with determination etched across his face.

"What time are you expecting Jamison?" I asked. While the jealousy remained held at bay, I was curious about the guy. I'd yet to ask Thatch about the man, so knew nothing about their history or even if there was one. Between the case dominating our lives and stealing time together, there was still so much left unknown. Not that I minded. I looked forward to getting to know Thatch so much better, and if I had my way, we'd have the rest of our days uncovering our histories.

Uncertainty passed across Thatch's eyes before he said, "I imagine a couple of hours." To be fair, my jealousy hadn't been exactly hidden, and his wariness, which I determined as being a sign of him being concerned about me, kinda got me all hot under the collar.

"That should be a fun meet," Kent said, her grin filled with sly amusement. She was such an arsehole.

"Kent," Thatch said, his voice firm, though I heard the tiredness creeping in the edges.

"What?" The innocence in her voice was bullshit.

"You shit-stirring for a reason?" I asked, wondering if she was aiming for something more than enjoying pissing me off. Not that I couldn't handle it. I gave her just as much crap.

Feigned nonchalance lifted her right shoulder in a careless shrug. "You entertain me," she said, her smile appearing alarmingly genuine. "And watching the big boss squirm is freakin' hilarious. He's never like this."

Something pretty close to pleasure rushed through me. After my and Thatch's connection and especially after finally sealing the deal, he was mine. It was as simple as that. And knowing others saw our bond, hell yes, there was a hit of pride pushing my damn chest out.

Michaels's voice startled me—and Kent, from her wide eyes and the fast twist of her neck. "Jenson owes me a hundred bucks." Tears sprang in his eyes for the barest of seconds before he seemed to get them under control. His sombre words pulled Kent and me up short. "He said you'd finally sort your shit out and get laid when you were going to see your niece." A small quirk of his lips and a shake of his head had him looking at me. "He'd be happy to know you figured it out."

I swallowed hard and sent him a nod. "We'll make them all pay."

Michaels dropped his head, took a breath, and then said, "I know," before returning his gaze to me.

A quick flick of my eyes to Thatch and my heart clenched. The stricken look on his face hurt my damn soul. "Lucas has something," he said.

"There's no official record of a sister." Lucas cast his eyes around the table. "There's one mention of a Marinda Brent connected to Jeramiah Brent twenty-three years ago. It was on a human police record in New Zealand, one for collecting a deceased's items."

My brows flew high. "How'd she die?"

"Shifter attack."

An ache ripped through my gut. An attack by a

shifter, while not unheard of, was rare. Shifters in animal form still had all their faculties, so there was no turning feral and losing one's mind. A shifter attacking and killing was the same as a human attacking and killing. If it was murder, then the murderer was a screwed-up piece of crap, just like every other murderer out there. The species didn't matter, except for the damage of the often unidentifiable remains left behind.

"Fuck" slipped past Thatch's lips.

"That fucking worthless—" Michaels jumped out of his seat, his chair slamming to the floor. "So his involvement is what, some sort of fucking vengeance or some shit?" Fury distorted his features, and his body practically vibrated. I expected the desire to shift and seek his own vengeance rode him hard. "Jenson was one of us, and fucking *human*." Spittle flew from Michaels's mouth.

My sister, Jenson, countless men, women, and children had been destroyed by the creation of drugs that were ruining thousands more lives, and the experimentation that went with it. Nausea swirled in my stomach. I exhaled hard before asking Lucas, "Was anyone charged?"

My question had him springing his face up and away from the screen. His eyes were wide. "No one was formally charged, but they had a name on the list but never received concrete evidence."

Loud pounding gathered in my head. I desperately wanted to close my eyes and block my ears, certain about what his next words would be.

"Lennon Blackheath."

And there it was.

"Fuck."

The room stilled for the barest of seconds before Kent's and Lucas's fingers flew over their keyboards. Meanwhile, Michaels legit snorted, drawing my attention to him.

His gaze met mine, a sardonic smile crossing his lips, his eyes still hard and distraught. "You know, we could just leave them to kill each other." A nonchalant shrug followed.

My gaze snapped to Thatch, almost tempted to agree and start talking him around, but he simply shook his head. "But Michaels has a point," I defended. "If Brent is in this whole thing to wipe out Blackheath, then we could let him have at it, right?" There was no remorse, no pang of longing for what could have or should have been. The world would be a better place once Lennon Blackheath was out of the picture. I had to hope the pack would dismantle after that. If not, I'd consider helping it along its way.

"And what about Lentwood?" Thatch challenged.

"We can hope he gets caught up in the crossfire but be prepared to step in and take him out. Blackheath will only be in this for the money. He's too damn stupid for anything bigger. Plus the fact that Lentwood is making this souped-up drug for vamps, its intent clearly to take down shifters and aim to perhaps adopt a more significant role for vampires, will have passed Blackheath by completely." Blackheath had no allegiance to anyone but himself. But he was also egotistical enough not to get involved in shifter trafficking if he knew the aim was to put shifters in the ground while vampires took dominion.

"No chance." Thatch crossed his large arms over his chest, the action drawing my eyes to his taut muscles in appreciation. When he spoke again, he drew my attention back to his face. "This whole operation with Lentwood is a shitshow. I seriously have no idea how he was able to stay under the radar for the two years when I was undercover. And that worries me. For all the situations that have gone wrong, especially recently, it means he's unreliable. We can't predict what his move is going to be beyond shipping out. Even then, we don't know for sure if he'll be at the dock."

I expelled a heavy, frustrated sigh. Thatch's words rang true, disappointingly so. Lentwood being a loose cannon was worrisome. "So, we move in and aim to take them all down."

"In an ideal world, yes. We also need to ensure we find any additional data of shifter experimentations and labs so no one is left behind, and no one can start this up again," Thatch clarified.

"When do we roll out?" Michaels stood, eagerness practically vibrating through him.

A quick glance at the clock, and Thatch said, "Roll out in twenty."

CHAPTER 12

Wide-eyed and with my heart stuttering, I allowed the scene to wash over me. In the single flickering light visible through the grimy window of the warehouse on the dock, I counted six bodies. That didn't mean they would be the only ones.

All prone forms were men, all in human form. Unsure of the cause of death, a bullet to their heads was likely. But what made me react was Lennon Blackheath. On his knees, bloody and cowering, he looked a far cry from the tyrant father and alpha I knew. A pang of foreign emotion hit me hard, making my hands shake and my breathing unsteady.

"Holy shit," Lucas whispered beside me.

I flinched at the sound of his voice, and my eyes

roamed the heavy fans and air ducts kicking out so much sound there was no chance anyone inside could hear us.

For a moment longer, I remained frozen, my blood turning to ice, still unsure how to react. What was the right response when you saw your father about to die? The same man who'd brutalised me as a child, as well as countless others?

"Copy, Callen?" Thatch's voice came through the comms, and my heart stuttered to life.

"Yeah, copy."

"You have eyes on Lentwood?"

After glancing at Lucas, who shook his head, I answered, "That's a negative." With the whirl of the fans reaching my ears, I refocussed on what mattered, saying, "We've got eyes on Blackheath."

Dead silence followed. Surprised by the lack of response, I continued. "We haven't seen Brent yet, but my gut's saying here's here." While I hadn't discussed that with Lucas, he didn't offer any dispute. "There are six dead," I added.

Thatch's rich and familiar voice appeared, his tone holding a softness I wasn't prepared for when he asked, "He alive?"

"Barely." Matter-of-factly, the truth of the statement was out there, along with the unspoken answer to the question no one voiced: Would we be stepping in?

Unless it would help take Lentwood down, unless Blackheath's death interfered with the investigation, the answer would be a resounding no. In the quiet that followed, I knew gut-deep that Thatch wanted to ask, wanted my approval, even though it went against every protocol, and in many ways every instinct we had.

We all knew exactly what Blackheath was capable of—me more than anyone. But Thatch's concern for me was what drove the tension in the air, made it ripple and reassure me that after all the crap, he would be by my side and we'd make a go of life without this threat hanging over us.

Wanting to reassure him, I clarified, "We'll wait for your signal. We're good to hold." While we wanted both Brent and my dad, Lentwood was my mission. There was no way I'd be stepping in and potentially spooking Lentwood.

His response was immediate. "Okay. If anything changes, let us know."

"Roger that," I said with a grin and visualised him rolling his intense, gorgeous eyes at me.

"Shall we head to the next window?" Lucas gestured to our right.

With a nod and a quick scan of our surrounds, we dashed over to take another look. Lucas and I were focusing on the north and east walls of the large building situated within the dockyards. When we'd arrived at the ship still loading containers, we'd followed a human carrying firearms to this building. It hadn't taken us long to discover the scene we'd just shared with Thatch.

With the next room clear, we continued around, spotting two guards, but still no Brent or Lentwood. It was time to go high. Up the fire escape to the first floor, I tapped my comms. "Copy, Kent?"

"Yep, copy."

"Can you get eyes on the first floor? Any movement?" Remaining hunched low, grip on the handle, I waited for her go-ahead.

"Give me a second."

I kept my eyes on the door, trusting Lucas to have my back while we waited in silence. Despite the adrenaline pumping through my veins, calm eased through me. Completely in my element with the anticipation of taking down scumbags and kicking arse at the same time, I breathed easily, eager to get going.

"Callen." Kent's voice came over the comms.

"Copy."

"Two bodies three rooms to the east. There's movement at the south that you need to check out, Thatch," Kent added.

"Got it," Thatch said.

"Thanks," I added. With that, I signalled to Lucas to

open the door. Three steps later, we were inside and heading east. I checked my weapon, selecting the potent darts and making them active. While bullets would have been my preference, we still needed answers and locations. Dead bodies wouldn't be able to provide us with that. Our footsteps remained muffled by the industrial vents and fans as we headed through the first, then the second room. Stilling, I tilted my head, hearing muted voices. From what I could tell, it was two men shooting the shit.

As I signalled at Lucas to enter, Kent's "Wait," made me fist my hand. Both of us paused while we waited for further explanation. "Helicopter inbound."

We needed to make this fast. Clear this floor so we could get to the roof and who I hoped like hell was Lentwood. The spike of my heartbeat had me moving with the barest of signals to Lucas. Hard and fast.

Ducking low as I edged around the corner, I saw two humans with their backs to us, chatting while staring through the window. Their mundane chatter reached my ears, *Lentwood* and *psycho wolf* two words that filtered through. The distinctive sound of rotor blades overhead gave us the extra muffler needed to head in closer. Lucas counted down with the slightest shift of his fingers. At one, we both fired, the darts hitting their marks and the two men hitting the floor.

Hurrying over, we ensured they were secure with cable ties, then hauled their prone forms to the side out of sight.

"Roof?" I aimed a pointed look at Lucas, almost challenging him to try to head to the ground floor first.

After he took a hard look at me, he nodded and checked in with Thatch. "Copy, Thatch. We're heading to the roof."

"Copy that," Thatch responded immediately. "Kent, do you have a visual on Lentwood?" Anticipation weaved through his question.

"No one's exited the helicopter yet. I'll let you know as soon as I have a visual." Kent cut off, and I sighed in annoyance.

"Thatch, what's your status?" While working with Lucas made absolute sense since we knew each other so well and had spotted each other on countless missions, being apart from Thatch was as much a blessing as a curse.

"We've just got eyes on Brent. He's heading towards the room where Blackheath is."

Divide and conquer. It appeared the only way to go.

"There's an SUV coming in fast. Still about five minutes out. Not sure who it is other than it jumped on our radar and seems to be on a mission to break every traffic rule going," Kent said, adding a new level of urgency to the moment.

"Got it." I nodded at Lucas, and we headed towards the staircase that would take us to the roof.

The sound of Lucas changing the setting on his firearm had me reacting in kind. All set with live ammo, we paused at the door. Lucas tapped on his thigh, drawing my attention. "We need whoever's in that helicopter to get out. If it's Lentwood, we can't give him the opportunity to escape."

He was right. Short of shooting at the rotor mast and stopping the helicopter from taking off, no bright ideas came to mind. "I suppose winging it is out of the question?"

His response was a snort.

Not knowing of any other way, side by side, we headed outside, keeping down and immediately dropping behind the large venting system. With the helicopter in sight, I angled as much as possible to check out the occupants, with zero success. At least the blades were still. There was no update from Kent nor Thatch, nor did sounds of fighting reach us, but that didn't mean anything considering the distracting noises in the warehouse. It meant we had no choice but to move out.

I nodded at Lucas. "You ready?" He bobbed his head in response. With a firm grip on my firearm, I made to the right, staying firmly behind the helicopter, Lucas behind me, and hoping like hell we were in the blind spot. Staying low and angling right as Lucas went left, we tore towards the doors. Loud pounding in my head guided my way, the handful of steps feeling like an eternity.

Gun aimed and steady, I stepped out of cover. My eyes widened, my gut dropping. Nausea battled for dominance, but screw that. Instead, my jaw clicked tight as I dropped the barest of gazes to my niece before settling on Lentwood.

There was no victory in his gaze. Simple curiosity greeted me.

I debated whether my shot would hit its mark before he could move, and with zero risk to Lucinda, who remained silent before him, her wide-eyed, frightened stare burning a hole in my chest, hitting my heart and making it stutter.

"You will not make the shot." His thick, accented voice startled me, but not enough to alter my aim.

I eventually found my voice—there was no way I could remain unaffected. Steel filled every syllable. "What are you expecting to happen here?" I wondered briefly about Koen, desperately hoping he wasn't dead. Then there was Lucas's safe house. He'd be pissed. With all the recent activity though, it wasn't that surprising infiltration was possible. Brent had the resources of the agency and there was no doubt he'd abuse them for his own gain.

"You're going to get in and give us safe passage to the ship."

His blatant disregard for the reality of this situation ripped a snort from me. An unpleasant grin lifted my lips and I shook my head, my hands remaining steady. "It's like you don't know me at all."

He quirked a brow at that. "You presume to think I give a shit about you and cared enough to find out who you are beyond that of an annoying bug?" Inflection filled his voice. Perhaps disbelief. Perhaps mere arrogance. The arsehole clearly didn't know me or understand just how fucking annoying I could be.

"Yet you cared enough to find my niece." I held my sneer at bay, and revelled in the flare of his eyes. Apparently, I rattled him more than he wanted to admit. I had no doubt my niece was targeted due to the possibility of her blood being just as special as my sister's. But there wasn't a chance he'd get the opportunity to test that out.

My smile turned sardonic as I weighed my options. The only thing I was certain about was that Lucinda would be getting off the helicopter alive on this rooftop while Lentwood would die. In my peripheral vision, another gun registered, this one aimed at Lucas. There was no doubt in my mind Lucas wouldn't waver. I also knew he'd wait for me to move.

"What are you hoping to achieve here?" I tried again. My gaze remained firm as I waited for him to answer. Apparently safe passage was one of his aims, but surely he didn't expect to get on to that ship.

"Your father underestimated you." Accusation carried his voice to me, filling me with a moment of pride that my dad being a piece of shit hadn't let me down. "He has no loyalty."

A derisive exhale burst out before I said, "You think?" Amusement lifted my words. "Yet you chose to get in bed with him." I gave the barest shake of my head. "It was clear you were smart, kept low and out of Thatch's path for so long, yet here you are...."

Narrowed eyes shot my way. "Here I am?"

The question was there, intended or not. "Brent's killing the bastard as we speak. Not quite sure what Brent's next move will be, but I don't think it will be to carry on with his plan to support this clusterfuck."

My finger begged to twitch. It would, but it wasn't quite time.

Finally a real reaction he couldn't hide as my words settled over him. The tension in his jaw set off dipped brows, where two lines formed between them. With a shift of his body as he became rigid, there was a widening of space between him and my niece. Barely two inches, but it would help.

A car's roaring engine made itself known. The reaction from Lentwood was all I needed. Whoever the occupants of the SUV were, Lentwood wasn't expecting them. A shadow, a flicker of uncertainty, was the prelude to "Seventeen" passing my lips, and my shot ringing out in almost perfect sync with Lucas's.

Before the number passed my lips, the round in the chamber already surging to life, my hand was out, reaching for Lucinda. The moment the bullet hit Lentwood square between the eyes, just as his eyes returned to me and away from the direction of the unannounced engine, my grip on Lucinda tightened and I hauled her to safety. I angled around, putting her out of harm's way as my gun held steady. The metal in his brain would incapacitate but not kill. As far as I was concerned, it was time to call in Durrant.

Thatch.

The squeal of tires and his following shout pierced the air. I needed to get to him. A sniff had me finally glancing away from the two forms slumped over in the helicopter. Lucinda's head was buried against my chest as she clung to me like a koala. Shudders wracked her body. My heart lurched, understanding her fear. I felt it all too closely. When I'd first spotted her next to Lentwood, I hadn't had the time for anything beyond reacting and neutralizing the situation. Now, with her terror pulsing through her, the reality of how close I'd come to losing her too had me lowering my gun, tucking it away, and folding her into my arms.

I breathed her in, hushed her as best as I could before finally risking a glance at Lucas. The human pilot was dead, and Lentwood cuffed. It would take a while before he woke. Though, after today's events as well as the years of torture he'd committed and lives he'd taken, I wasn't sure if he'd ever be given the opportunity.

"You go. I'll call this in." Lucas placed a finger to his ear to direct Kent before saying, "Comms are down." A sneer followed before he pulled out his phone to call Kent. Worry edged into my gut that somehow these guys had been savvy enough to cut our communication. That was my cue. With a pounding heart, I turned and took the steps needed to get off the roof. To get to Thatch. Comms down was not good.

With still no idea of what I'd find on the lower levels or what had taken place, I loosened one hand from my niece and rearmed myself. Through the door and heading down the steps, I paused at the heavy pounding of footsteps.

"Let me the fuck go. I need to get to that damn

roof." An "oomph" and a heavy thud followed Thatch's growled words.

"Christ, calm down. I heard at least a couple of shots." This voice I vaguely recognised. "The chopper hasn't started back up either."

Thatch's growl erupted. I reacted to the sound by charging down the steps and dashing across the hallway. There was no way I could call out and make my presence known, not until I had eyes on the situation and had made sure Lucinda was safe.

The growling stopped, no doubt at the sound of my descent.

"Callen." It seemed Thatch had no such concerns. A grin pulled across my mouth. It meant he was safe.

Down the last flight of stairs I went. My gaze fell on Thatch, whose eyes were already locked in my direction. Relief surged through me, caressing every inch of my skin, my limbs, my heart. He was safe. Then my eyes narrowed on the hands gripping him—one on his bicep, the other on his chest.

The growl tore from my throat, feral and instinctive. Immediately, the blond released him, his hands pulling up in the air, his gesture placating. The grin on his face though would have given me pause if it wasn't for the surprise and concern flickered in Thatch's gaze when his eyes landed on my niece. They roamed a moment before landing on me. I offered a reassuring smile and slight nod, trying to let him know she was okay.

The barest of moments later, heat pressed against me.

Air filled my lungs as I also inhaled Thatch's sent. He was safe, and holding on to both me and Lucinda, his face pressed against my neck. The closeness, the touch, the complete sense of rightness flowed through me, relaxing my muscles, and in response, Lucinda's soft sobs calmed, her shuddering abating.

Thatch leaned back. He spared me a glance, his deep brown eyes alight with those flecks of green that always drew me in, before his eyes landed on Lucinda. After pressing a light kiss to her head and whispering, "You're safe, baby girl," he closed his mouth over mine. At the contact, my heart steadied out, no longer as frantic as I worried about the two people in my life who held my heart. Slow and soft, our lips touched for the smallest of moments. Thatch pulled away, and while I wanted nothing more than to clasp him to me, not only did we have an audience, but in the next room, the scent of blood was strong. I needed my niece away from this place.

Not ready to tear my eyes away from Thatch just yet, I spoke directly to him. "Lucas is speaking to Kent and getting this called in to Durrant."

A curt nod and the softness in his eyes edging away meant boss man Thatch was back. He flicked his gaze to Lucinda and raised a questioning brow. Koen. I knew what he asked. But I had no answers and talking to the girl in my arms right now wasn't the best idea.

I shrugged, saying, "Lucas will speak to Kent and find out what happened." Since we'd been in contact with Kent the majority of the time during the mission, it remained unclear how Lentwood had managed to infiltrate and get his hands on my niece. I swallowed thickly as I glanced towards the doorway where I knew there were bodies—and somewhere close by was Lennon Blackheath.

The whole time, Thatch's attention was on me. He watched my movement closely, then shook his head, answering my unspoken question of whether my father was alive. There would be no mourning for the deadbeat I shared my genes with. While I wouldn't be celebrating either, I welcomed the sliver of peace settling in my soul.

He wouldn't be able to hurt anyone ever again.

"Brent?" I asked, indicating to a different doorway and another exit to leave the warehouse.

"Out of action." Thatch's shoulder brushed mine as we walked. "Lent—"

"The same." A grim satisfaction weaved its way through me.

"You know"—the voice stopped me in my tracks—"it's a bit freakin' weird how you two have whole conversations without saying a whole lot."

Thatch shook his head as I angled towards the man who'd had his hands on Thatch.

"Jamison?" I gave him a quick once over and grinned, immediately knowing there was no way he and Thatch had indulged in anything. Not that he wasn't a good-looking guy. But it was more than Thatch's frustrated eye-rolls when he spoke to him that tipped me off. The blond-haired pretty panther was not his type.

Jamison returned my smile, his eyes alight with humour and friendliness. "One and the same." His gaze roamed over the three of us before he said, "We'll catch up later, and I'm sure I can tell you some stories about Thatch that will have you pissing your pants." He waggled his brows, the gesture so ridiculously out of place with the coppery scent of blood growing more oppressive by the second. I liked the guy immediately.

"Sounds good." I gripped Thatch's hand, the move still unfamiliar but the touch perfectly natural. Together, we headed out to the fresh air to await Durrant's questions and make sure that now that the key players were finally out of the picture, every single lab—both for experimentation and production—was burned to the ground.

CHAPTER 13

"Unbelievable." Lucas shook his head at me.

Kent simply grinned. "This is going to go so badly."

Thatch looked on, amused... or perhaps it was closer to perplexed. Though, I wasn't quite sure why, since he knew all the details already.

"What?" I shrugged, not seeing the big deal. At first, I'd admittedly had the exact same reactions as all three of them when Durrant had pulled me into her office three days after the shitshow that had gone down.

In that time, I'd organized childcare and agreed to move in with Thatch permanently, though truth be told, I'd had no intentions of moving out even if Thatch hadn't made it official and asked for Lucinda and me to move in for good. On top of that, there was a large-scale task force working on rescuing the few shifters who'd still been imprisoned, while shutting down all the research and production lines to get all traces of the drug off the streets.

There was real progress, and after my conversation with Durrant, we'd agreed to me having a couple of weeks off to settle Lucinda, then I'd be starting my new job.

SICB division manager. On top of the varying emotions that had torn through me at the offer, of course battling with the stroking of my healthy ego, I'd legit laughed. Durrant hadn't.

"But why?" There was genuine confusion in Lucas's question. No jealousy or spite, just genuine bewilderment.

I cocked my brow. "Because I'm badass." I barely kept the "dur" out of my voice.

Thatch shook his head. "Just tell him."

He was no fun. I'd already had this discussion with Thatch. He could have at least given me the chance to wind Lucas up some more.

"Do you mean, why not you?"

"No," Lucas said immediately, while Kent said, "Exactly that," at the same time.

I shot her an unimpressed look before admitting, "I did actually say that to Durrant."

Lucas eased back in his chair a little now the initial shock of my promotion had sunk in. "And what did she say?"

The shit-eating grin on my face was immediate. "That she wants to see you in forty-five minutes."

Tension had Lucas's neck straining. "What for?"

I gave a careless shrug. I totally knew, but when Durrant threatened me with extra paperwork if I opened my mouth, I believed her. The woman was not to be crossed. To be honest, we were all somewhat flummoxed by her calm acceptance of what had gone down and how we'd kept everything over the past few days off the radar.

Lucas groaned. "Fine."

With my gaze moving to Thatch, I darted my brows up and down. If he shared his news, it would become quite clear the direction Lucas's meeting would take. The difference was, no one was confirming or denying anything, which meant I wouldn't be buried under paperwork.

"Really?" Thatch said and slowly shook his head despite the humour lighting his eyes. "Michaels, get your arse in here so I don't have to repeat myself."

A heavy sigh preceded Michaels's booted footsteps. The levity in the room shifted slightly. Michaels was still struggling with the loss of Jenson. We all were, but he bore the loss heavily.

Once seated, Michaels gave a chin lift and then a small smile when Kent called him a loser. The sight eased an ache in my chest. I understood loss all too well. And that small gesture meant he wasn't lost. Michaels would bounce back.

Thatch leaned against the table, his hands to the side of him gripping the metal top. My heart lurched a little at the nervous glance he cast my way. I offered him a wink. He had this. It was a big deal and a move that surprised the hell out of me. The gesture behind it was an additional reason why I wouldn't be letting this man go. Ever.

"I've agreed to take on a new position."

Kent's eyes sprang wide, and for the first time since I'd known her, she appeared to be rendered speechless. I'd have to give Thatch a high five later for that accomplishment. Meanwhile, Michaels's head dropped. Thatch had been concerned about his reaction, how he'd handle the double loss, but he'd also been the one to convince himself and me that this was a move for us... and Lucinda.

"I'm taking over the position as head trainer at the SICB Academy."

Kent snorted, Michaels's head shot up, and Lucas had to grab on to the table to stop himself from toppling over in his chair. I ignored them all, my focus on Thatch and looking for any tells that he regretted his decision. When his eyes flicked to mine, a full smile lifted his lips, and his wink would have had my knees going weak if I wasn't made of tougher stuff. Admittedly, sitting down helped.

"Holy crap, you're serious." Kent was the first to respond.

"Yeah." He nodded. "Being the head of our unit has been an honour, but it's time I stayed closer to home." He didn't cast a look my way; he didn't need to. It was probably best he didn't either, as there was no way I'd let Kent catch me gushing over his proclamation.

Lucas sat forward as he spoke. "So you're both stepping out of the field?"

"There are times I may need to step up," I said, "but we have Lucinda now." She'd lost so much. I couldn't allow her to go through anything like that again. Or I'd try my hardest not to.

Lucas nodded his understanding, his eyes returning to Thatch as his eyes widened. There it was. The understanding that Durrant would be offering Lucas Thatch's position. He composed himself immediately, the epitome of togetherness. But I knew better. Despite his many years on this earth, he'd be bouncing around like a baby joey inside.

"There's a lot more to discuss and work out,"

Thatch said in the quiet that followed. "I have a few weeks before the move, but we'll get it figured out, okay?" His eyes fell to Michaels, who finally looked up and nodded.

A moment later, Michaels stood, stepped forward, and clasped Thatch's hand, tugging him into a hug. "I'm happy for you."

I watched as Thatch tightened his grip, then looked away, giving them some time.

Lucas stood, clapping me on the shoulder. Amusement coloured his words. "Who'd have thought Callen 'pain in the arse' Blackheath would be stepping up in the world?" He bumped my shoulder. "I'm happy for you, man. Seriously."

"Thanks."

"And you have a couple of weeks off now?"

"Yeah. I need to spend some time with Lucinda, get to know her better, work out schooling and stuff."

Lucas nodded. "And how's Koen doing?"

I grinned. The young shifter was as tough as they came. He'd been injured and rendered unconscious when Lucinda had been taken. They'd been in the small courtyard playing basketball, out of Kent's loop. And to be fair, she had been running the whole mission, so her sole focus was on the docks. "He's doing well. Back at ours. Healing. Going stir-crazy. He's also applied to the

SICB Academy." And I had no doubts he would excel. He was a good kid, resilient and loyal as hell. And me figuring that out after knowing the guy for less than a week was saying something.

"Huh. That's good. Thatch will make a warrior out of him," he teased, making me laugh.

A small glance at Thatch, and he nodded, ready to go too. "We're heading out. Michaels." I held out my palm and shook his hand, pulling him into a tight hug. "I'm just a call away," I said quietly, needing him to know that while our immediate working relationship had come to an end, I didn't want it to end there.

He gave me a tight nod when he pulled away. "We'll catch up soon and shoot the shit," he offered.

A grin spread across my mouth. "Sounds good." My gaze travelled to Kent, whose scowl dipped her brow low. "Just get your arse over here, woman."

I think she surprised the hell out of the both of us when she did just that. "This doesn't mean I like you, man." Her hold was strong when she wrapped her arms around me.

I grunted my laugh. "You're going to miss me so damn much."

She pulled away, the scowl that she must have dropped when hugging me taking a moment to reform on her features. "Like a hole in the head."

"You're on child-sitting duties soon, so it won't be too long before I get to piss you off again."

"Fucking Jada," she grumbled.

I pressed a quick kiss on the top of her head, then jumped out of reach before she could bust my balls.

Lucas's hand reached for mine. "I'll call you tomorrow." A tight, quick hug followed before he backed away and headed to his workstation.

I owed Lucas so much. He'd put everything at risk for Lucinda and me. Thank Christ it had paid off.

"Ready?" Thatch was at my side, his heat welcoming.

"Absolutely."

"Seriously, just get the hell out of here already. How the hell am I supposed to talk shit about you both with you still here?" Kent threw me a wink at the same time she flipped me the bird.

Hand in hand, Thatch and I turned towards the exit and left for home, me hollering over my shoulder, "Love you too, woman."

It didn't take long before we were heading through the main gates of Thatch's place, now officially my home too. Just last night, I'd finally met Mary, his amazing housekeeper, and I'd seen Bert again, who was assisting more with Lucinda and Koen, especially for setting

Lucinda up with clothes and whatever else she needed to make her room her own.

Koen had taken the small guest house that was to the west of the property, giving him some separation, but close enough should we need each other.

"They seemed to take that well." Needless to say, Thatch had had some concerns about how his team would take him stepping down once he'd decided to take on the new role at the academy.

"Lucas is a good guy. They'll do well together." He offered me a lopsided grin. "Obviously he's not me."

I laughed. "That he's not." I leaned over the console and pressed my lips to his. "Not quite sure there's another like you."

His dark eyes scanned mine, those tiny specks of green bright in the afternoon sun. "Best not forget that either."

"As if you'd let me forget." I rolled my eyes and reached for the door handle.

"Do you fancy a shift and a run?"

His request took me by surprise. Immediately, warmth spread through me. Thatch had taken to his new shifter self with such ease. I loved seeing him in wolf form. "I'd like that."

He grinned. "I just need to talk to Mary. Do you

want to get Lucinda and perhaps Koen? It'll help him, right?"

I nodded, my heart full from this man's thoughtfulness. He did this whole family thing and caring for others stuff so much better than I did.

"What?" he asked, and I realised I'd been silently staring at the dude like a goof.

"Just thinking how hot you are."

His brow quirked. "No, you weren't."

A snort escaped me before I admitted, "Well, I *do* think that all the time, but I'm just... er... happy, I guess." I rolled my eyes at myself.

Thatch's smirk came quickly. "You guess?"

"Yeah." I shook my head at him. "You know you're God's gift to shifters and all that jazz."

"All that jazz? Is there something we need to discuss?" he sassed.

"Piss off," I said with a grin.

"Speaking of things to discuss, ABBA?"

I snorted. Maybe one day I'd treat him to a replay, complete with white spandex and a beard. For the moment, distraction would have to do. "I love your sexy arse and am more than okay that you're mine."

Heat filled Thatch's gaze, and he tugged my hand from the door so I fully faced him. "Just so we're clear, I love your fine arse just as much. And you're mine, too."

"Goo—"

The word wasn't quite out of my mouth before his lips pressed against mine. An intensity that I'd only known with him beat a rhythm through my heart, taking residence there. This was what love and family was, should be, would forever be if I had my way. I clung tightly to the emotion. Imprinted it to memory. Yeah, there was no chance in hell I'd be letting go of my shifter. Ever.

I HOPE YOU HAPPY SIGHED! BE SURE TO CHECK out WEAKER THAN INSTINCT, book two. Continue reading for a sneak peek.

CHAPTER ONE

Michaels

Wedged to the ground, I took stock of my limbs. Wriggling toes. Flexing fingers. Cracking neck as I turned it left, then right. Three good things going for me. Shoulders— there was no holding back the grunt of pain tearing out of me.

Red hot and intense, agony sliced through my stomach, my side. I screwed up my eyes, willing my breaths to even.

One breath. Two. All the way up to five before it was time to assess the situation.

I pried my eyes open and squinted through the smoke-filled air.

Debris surrounded me, disorientating and chaotic. Lucas was going to kick my arse. There were no ifs, buts, or maybes.

Obviously I'd heal. My shifter abilities came in super handy, but the blazing ache on my right-hand side couldn't be magicked or wished away.

Focussed on slow and steady exhales, I guided my hand to the area, already guessing what I'd find. A heavy sigh, followed by another throb of pain, trickled free when my palm connected with wet metal.

Blood. The sticky liquid coated the steel, the metallic scent thick and cloying.

Impaled was never a good look, let alone an ideal situation. But I wasn't dead, so there was that.

My comms sparked to life. "Michaels, this is Kent. Check in. Over."

Biting back my urge to grunt as I moved to touch the small device in my ear, I held my breath and finally pressed the button. "Michaels checking in. Over." With no quiver, no shake, my tone remained neutral, controlled.

The two-second beat before Kent's voice sounded in my ear was enough to warn me that she knew that shit had hit the fan. Her instincts were spookily accurate, even when a hundred kilometres away. "Status report. Over." There it was—her tight voice, her tone making it clear I should be more concerned about her kicking my arse rather than Mathew Lucas, the head of the ITU, the Infiltration Tactical Unit I was a member of.

"I may need an assist. Over." I wasn't quite gung-ho enough to think I could pull the steel out of myself. Well, not without causing more injuries. The thought of taking longer to heal, which meant more time out of the field, was enough for me to admit I needed backup.

Kent didn't hold back her pissed-off snarl. "Two minutes. Over and out."

Yeah, Kent was definitely the vampire I should be more concerned about.

Waiting out the two minutes wasn't a hardship. The explosion had killed Muerso. The pool of blood decorated with ash and debris, as well as his prone form, was all the confirmation I needed. Plus the explosion was directly linked to the computer systems. I expected that would annoy Kent, our department whiz at all things cyber, but Muerso's death would put an end to his criminal dealings.

Three months of intel told me he hadn't been part of a wider ring. And with his servers destroyed, it was one more shady criminal enterprise dismantled. The metal piercing my side was totally worth it.

"You look like shit." Chris's grin was wide as he stepped carefully over the debris. His attention drifted to Muerso's motionless form before returning to me, his brow quirked high. "I take it you not waiting for your team was worth it?"

I studied him closely, assessing if he was as annoyed as Kent. With his grin still in place, his posture relaxed, he seemed okay, but as he crouched before me and prodded my wound, I reconsidered my evaluation.

There was no holding back my hiss at his touch. Narrowing my eyes, I stared hard, holding back my snarl.

"You're meant to wait for your partner." His dark eyes appeared black in the flickering lights and the smoke that had yet to settle.

I rolled my eyes, which did nothing to ease the guilt bubbling to life in my gut. "You were warned I was an arsehole in the first five minutes of joining the team," I grumbled.

"True, but you seem determined to push your reputation into uncharted waters. Putting yourself at risk like this is bullshit." The calm tone, the casual way he scanned me for further injuries, didn't gel with his words or the hardening glint in his gaze.

"Sorry. The wanker in me is strong."

Chris's lips twitched.

"While I'm digging the kebab look, you know, the

whole wolf-on-a-skewer thing, you wanna help un-stab me?" I worked hard at controlling my expression, my voice. The injury in my side was a constant pulse of agony, and the sooner I was free, the sooner I could get pain meds and heal. While I was a legit arsehole lately, like right now for heading into the building without Chris, my partner of six months, I wasn't a masochist.

I wasn't that at all, and everyone in the team knew it, even Chris, the newest enforcer to join our unit.

At the sound of leather soles on rubble, he glanced behind him when a couple of medics entered, giving them a nod. "Looks like we can un-skewer you." With an effortless grace I was envious of right now, Chris stood and made room for Grace and Hansen.

The two medics made quick work of checking that pulling me from the steel was the best way to tackle my release, and within a few minutes, the three of them yanked me free. Chris took a little too much pleasure in my grunt and groan.

"Fuck." Lightheaded and shaky, I trembled, wavering on my feet. Hansen stopped me from face-planting by putting a strong arm around me. My head swam, a fresh wave of agony rolling through me and turning my stomach.

I swallowed hard. No way would I vomit. I'd never live it down. Chris would waste no time at all spreading that story about me in the unit. Would I deserve the shit talk? Absolutely. No chance would I make it easy for him, though.

"Let's get you a stretcher," Hansen said.

"Nuh-uh. I can walk."

The three of them rolled their eyes. Not that I gave two shits. The investigation was over. The crim was dead—honestly, the best place for the blood dealer. As far as I was concerned, this was a win.

Directing me forward, Chris tugged out his phone, beginning to record the mass of devastation I'd caused. "Kent is going to go for your jugular, man."

Not bothering to glance back as I unsteadily stepped over the rubble, trying not to stumble, I shrugged. "There might be something salvageable." There so wasn't anything left that could be rescued from the burst of flames and mini-explosions I'd detonated earlier.

Chris's snort called bullshit.

Ignoring him, I made it outside to the waiting ambulance. With blood trickling down my side and seeping into my tactical pants, I couldn't risk not getting patched up. I clambered into the open back, Grace following me inside.

"You need me to cut your shirt off?"

Wide-eyed, I stared at her in horror. "Fuck no."

Her lips thinned out as she waited for me to unfasten

my bulletproof vest and tug off my black SICB-issued T-shirt. These things were expensive as hell. The Supernatural Investigation & Crime Bureau budget was shit, and our unit's even worse, which meant if I wrecked the damn thing, I'd have to buy a new one.

Screw that. I'd wait till my yearly replacements.

By the time I eased the bloody shirt off, sweat trickled down my temples and my spine. A hot shower, a coffee, maybe some whiskey, probably a few stitches to help the wound along its way, and I'd be golden.

"Oh fucking hell." A gaping hole from the skewer had destroyed my shirt. I flicked my attention to Grace, who remained stoic as she stared at me, no doubt thinking I was a prize dickhead. "You could have told me it was wrecked." Petulance rumbled through my voice.

"Could I?" she deadpanned, swiping up some medical supplies so she could clean me up.

Keeping my mouth shut as she dabbed at my wound, I grimaced, knowing better than to complain. A wince and a hiss escaped as she cleansed the wound, and I glanced away quickly.

"You need an injection to numb the area?"

"I'm good," I said tightly, earning myself a grunted mumble about me being a pain in the arse. This wasn't Grace's first rodeo of stitching me up, especially over the past year. If I were her, I'd be sick of me too.

A few stitches later and a bandage taped on, I was good to go.

"I'll be happy if I don't see you again." Grace shot me a pointed look, and Hansen snorted as he closed the rear doors of the ambulance.

"You won't miss me?" I tugged on a fresh tee that was shoved at me by Hansen. Unfortunately, not a new SICB one I could steal.

"Miss your surly arse? Hell no." She followed up with a smirk.

I waved her off, giving my thanks to both of them before seeking out Chris. Already in his car, he was tapping his fingers to whatever bad-taste beat was playing on the radio.

"You done?"

"Yeah."

He bobbed his head. "I've asked Tony to take your vehicle back to the main headquarters." Meaning, as opposed to our unit's covert location. "Thought it would give you a chance to heal before you head out later."

It would be easier if Chris was a dickhead. It would mean I could keep my distance and not like the man, but when he did stuff like this, it made it tricky. "Thanks," I grumbled, settling down in the passenger seat. "You get my bag?"

He snorted. "You mean the one that's burned to a crisp?" The sound of the engine cut through his chuckle. "That'd be a no."

"Damn it. I liked that bag. It had my favourite Beretta in it." What a clusterfuck. I secured my seatbelt, readjusting the belt strap so it didn't press down on my injury. Not only would I be getting a bollocking from Lucas, but I'd destroyed my bag and one of my handguns.

But at least the bad guy was toast, and I could close my eyes for a few minutes while Chris drove us to the ITU headquarters.

Or maybe not.

Barely sitting up straight in the SUV, I grimaced as Chris took each turn fifteen kilometres faster than necessary. Despite his smile and ease with handling this situation, and the several others since he joined the ITU, the lion was pissed off.

I got it. Deserved it. Absolutely understood it.

Since Jenson's—my old partner's—death last year, I hadn't made life easy for myself or my team. I kept pushing the boundaries and had been reprimanded more than once for taking unnecessary risks. Add to that the number of times I'd gone lone wolf, and I was surprised I still had a job.

That I did such things, was so selfish at times, didn't

sit easy. But I didn't know how to stop, how to process Jenson no longer being around. And no amount of talking about it, including the mandatary six sessions of therapy after the whole Lentwood shitshow, changed that one bit.

It didn't help that I'd refused to share a single thing the whole time. Well, nothing of value or truth.

"You doing okay there?"

I tilted my head to look at Chris and offered a chin lift. "Still alive."

He grunted in response.

"You got something to say?"

He sent a quick glance my way. "Not sure there's any point." His gaze returned to the road ahead.

The headlights caught on the late-night mist that had settled over Sydney. I always liked this time of night, especially on a weeknight. The busy city was virtually still with most residents tucked up for the night, ready for their early starts in the morning. So close to the head-quarters, it was especially quiet.

While I registered Chris's words, I struggled to form a response that wouldn't simply piss him off even further. Landing on "Fair enough," I watched as the elec-tronic gates whirled into action at the compound and thought about the report Lucas would demand I write.

We pulled into the underground parking, and Chris

found a space and parked. I exited with a grunt, irritating my injury.

"Get to the infirmary. You're going to need all the strength you can get before Lucas sees you."

Not wanting to rile Chris up any more, I held back my refusal, since I'd already been patched up. Though some drugs that actually blurred the edges of my pain wouldn't go amiss. "He really that upset?"

His brows shot high. "I don't think upset quite covers it."

With a nod of thanks and a grimace, I waved off his help and headed to see the doc.

It didn't take too long to get the all clear—after having a couple of shards of metal pulled out of my back, which I hadn't noticed before—and make my way to the central workspace. This was really Kent's domain, and she was the first to spot me.

"You know what they call a dead shifter who goes in blind and plays with metal sticks?" Kent deadpanned, her unwavering attention on me.

Knowing not to bait the vampire, I simply looked at her.

"Whatever the fuck they want because the cockhead is dead." Her stare was hard, the only tell she gave that she wanted to lay me out.

I sighed, hating the guilt raising its ugly head.

When Jenson had been killed by our former division manager, it shook the whole team, devastated us all. Despite knowing how much it had impacted everyone, I found it easier to not focus on any of it. It hurt too fucking much otherwise. "I'm sorry I was a cockhead."

An unimpressed grunt filled the space as Kent narrowed her eyes at me. "Stop trying to get dead."

"That's not what—"

"Michaels, office, now." Lucas's usually quiet, steady voice was tense and filled with ice. My attention still on Kent, I widened my eyes.

The vamp simply smirked at me and flipped me off. "Enjoy getting your arse handed to you."

Locking my jaw, I shot her a stink eye, which only had her chuckling as I made my way to Lucas's open door. The man was at his desk, his focus on me as I loosened my limbs, trying not to appear affected.

"Close the door and sit."

Read what happens next in Michaels's story, WEAKER THAN INSTINCT.

Acknowledgments

I've really ventured into new territory with *Thicker Than Water*. Halfway through I stopped writing and abandoned this book for about three months. Even though this felt like a story that simply must be written, I faltered, admittedly frightened that fans of my contemporary romance wouldn't be keen.

It was only when so many readers reached out to me with so much positivity from my last release, that I worked up the courage to pick this back up and continued to write.

Thank you, reader, for being kind and generous with your praise. Without you, this manuscript would likely have gathered dust for a wee bit longer. I appreciate your support so much.

A FEW EXTRA SHOUTOUTS:

My bestie at BookSmith Design has once again rocked my cover. She really is such an incredible cheerleader of mine.

There's not been a day in my life that I didn't know my parents were proud of me. I'm grateful for their support, their love, and am so lucky that we're also such amazing friends too.

Donna, my wifey, my friend, my sanity, you are my rock.

Louisa Masters, my sister author, you're my favourite person to share cocktails with. I'm so thankful to have you as such an incredible friend.

Ink-N-Flow simply rock. Our weekly calls, the loo breaks usually because the *Jizz and Shat* show is on form makes my week. I adore you, ladies.

A special shoutout to Annette B. Thank you for being such an incredible human being. Your friendship, your individuality, your absolute kick-arse self have had such an impact on me and my own world. I am grateful to call you a friend.

And finally, my boys. You are my world.

About the Author

Becca Seymour lives and breathes all things book related. Usually with at least three books being read and two WiPs being written at the same time, life is merrily hectic. She tends to do nothing by halves, so happily seeks the craziness and busyness life offers.

Living on her small property in Queensland with her human family as well as her animal family of cows, chooks, sheep, and dogs, Becca appreciates the beauty of the world around her and is a believer that love truly is love.

To check for updates head to Becca's website:
HTTPS://BECCASEYMOUR.COM
You can sign up for her newsletter here:
HTTPS://LANDING.MAILERLITE.COM/WEBFORMS/
LANDING/R9FOI4
Plus, join her Facebook group, which she shares with the awesome Louisa Masters here:
HTTPS://WWW.FACEBOOK.COM/GROUPS/
SEYMOURBOOKSWITHMASTERFULMEN/

facebook.com/beccaseymourauthor

twitter.com/beccaseymour_

instagram.com/authorbeccaseymour

bookbub.com/authors/becca-seymour

tiktok.com/@beccaseymourwrites